Ben Fox:

Squirrel Zombie Specialist at Your Service

SPENCER HILL
MIDDLE GRADE

Contact: Spencer Hill Press, PO Box 247, Contoocook, NH 03229, USA

Please visit our website at www.spencerhilmiddlegrade.com

Whitney, Daisy, 1972

Ben Fox: Squirrel Zombie Specialist at Your Service :
a novel / by Daisy Whitney - 1st ed.
p. cm.

Summary: To save his dog, a ten-year-old boy must battle squirrel
zombies his cat has raised in the backyard.

The author acknowledges the copyrighted or trademarked status and
trademark owners of the following wordmarks mentioned in this
fiction: Academy Award, Barbie, Benadryl, Calvin and Hobbes, Doritos,
Face Chat, Frisbee, Goosebumps, Jedi, Monopoly, Snow White, Super
Glue, Swiss Army, Triumph, Velcro, World Series, YouTube, Ziploc

Cover design and interior illustrations by Slake Saunders
Interior layout by Jennifer Carson

ISBN: 9781939392190 (paperback)
ISBN: 9781939392206 (ebook)

Printed in the United States of America

This story is dedicated to my son
who imagined it with me.

1

The Thing About Cats

Let me just say, for the record, that I liked cats.

But I didn't entirely understand them.

Take my cat Percy.

Sometimes, when I woke up in the middle of the night, I'd find him staring at me. A cold hard stare, like he was looking inside me and knew all the secrets of my ten-year-old soul.

He also spent his days pacing from room to room as he meowed loud and cranky-sounding meows. At nothing. At walls. At doors. At pieces of furniture.

Was there a reason for this weirdness?

I didn't know. I couldn't figure him out.

I especially didn't know why he was so destructive. He'd jump on the kitchen counter, swish his tail from side to side, and knock off plates, cups, once even a glass bowl, which we found shattered on the floor when we came home from seeing a movie about talking dogs. It was almost as if he relished breaking things, like a rock-star cat trashing a hotel room. Right before the school year started last month, he knocked Ms. Fitzgibbon's miniature frog collection off her porch railing. Ms. Fitzgibbon marched up to our front door with a plastic bag full of broken frog statues and demanded payment. "Your dastardly Siamese cat maimed my prized ceramic frog collection, and it will cost one hundred and twenty dollars and twenty-two cents to replace my little green beauties," she'd said to my mom, who'd stifled a laugh at those last three words.

Percy smashed picture frames, too. I once saw him bat a picture frame with his paw, knocking it over. Was it just a coincidence that the frame happened to hold a photo of the dog?

But the thing I really couldn't understand about Percy was why he wasn't nice to our dog, Captain Sparkles. He hissed at her, unsheathed his claws, and refused to play chase with her. Which made no sense because Captain Sparkles was (and still is) the nicest, sweetest, smartest, most awesome dog in the universe. A black and white lab/border collie mix—named for the YouTube celebrity but without the Z—she had the softest black fur, the cutest white paws, and the biggest brown eyes. She could also sit, stay, shake, and catch a Frisbee in mid-air. She loved to fetch tennis balls, and she could do this for hours in the backyard or the park. My mom and dad had taught her all those tricks, but someday I was going to teach her stuff too because I planned to be a dog trainer.

That was the other thing about cats. As far as I could tell, you couldn't train them. They didn't listen. They didn't learn. And they just wreaked havoc. Like the time Percy raised an entire army of zombie squirrels right in my backyard. It took me the longest time to figure out why Percy unleashed a squadron of former roadkill on his family.

But once I understood, everything I knew about cats and dogs changed, and this is the story of how it happened.

2 The Truth About Dog Doors

T hat Monday afternoon, I was finishing my math homework about those dreaded things known as fractions. Captain Sparkles was racing in and out through the dog door that had just been installed that day, and Percy was sound asleep on the living room couch, his paws sticking up in the air, his chubby belly moving up and down as he breathed. Captain Sparkles sprinted up to him and shook her stuffed duck toy in his face. That woke him up, and he gave her the evil eye, along with a screechy meow, before he unveiled a set of claws at her. Then he rolled over, stretched, and dragged his claws down the back of the couch to sharpen them.

"Percy, you need to use your scratching post," I scolded him. But he never listened. He hopped off the couch, landing right in front of Captain Sparkles. She dropped the toy and pounced on him. Percy hissed, then ran, and she barreled after him into the kitchen. The cat skidded into the wall, recovered, accelerated, and ran under the dining room table. He squeaked out a U-turn to double back into the living room, knocking over a plant on the coffee table. The dog caught up and cornered him by the couch. Percy cowered, and his sleek fur stood straight up, like a giant mohawk.

Then he yowled, loudly.

3

My mom appeared out of nowhere, as moms often do when trouble is brewing. She made her voice low, like a growling dog's, and said, "Off."

Captain Sparkles backed away, and my mom grabbed Percy and cradled him. She stood over the dog and said, "Captain, down now."

Instantly, Captain Sparkles plopped down on her side and laid her head on the hardwood floor. You could tell from the look in her eyes that she knew she was in trouble.

"Mom! How can you get mad at the dog? She just wants to play with the cat."

"And I don't think Percy wants to play with Captain Sparkles, so we have to give the dog boundaries," she said.

"What about Percy? Doesn't he need boundaries too?" I said as she handed me the cat.

"He's a cat, honey. They can't be trained like dogs," she said and she left the room.

Maybe I could train him though. I put Percy down in front of Captain Sparkles. "See, Captain. Here's Percy. He wants to be your friend."

Percy, evidently, had no interest in being friends. He hissed at her, which seemed a bit extreme to me. Her too, since she nipped his ear in response. Percy yowled, then bolted like he was on fire. But as he neared the back door, he looked back once, as if he were laughing. As if he had a cat secret. He practically vaulted through the dog door, the plastic flap hitting his fat, furry butt. Then he hurtled across the deck, which perched high above our back yard.

I watched him through the window as he disappeared into our steep, hilly yard. Then I finished my fractions, read my history assignment, had dinner, and went to bed.

I woke up around midnight when I heard a scratching sound. I glanced down at Captain Sparkles, who was conked out at the foot of my bed, all four legs up in the air.

I stretched forward to pet her belly. I've never been able to resist her, not since the day I'd found her picture on the local shelter's website and begged my parents to get her. She had been so tiny and cute in her puppy picture, weighing only twelve pounds. She's forty-eight pounds now, which means she quadrupled. Yeah, I kind of rule at math.

Just kidding about the math. It's my least favorite subject.

I tossed the covers aside and got out of bed. The lights were off in the house except for a horse-shaped nightlight in the bathroom for my sister, Macy. I peered into her bedroom. Macy looked like a starfish splayed out on her bed. Her floor was covered with soccer balls, bouncy balls, kickballs. She'd get in trouble in the morning for taking them out at night, but she'd just nod and claim she'd never do it again. Macy had perfected the smile-and-nod technique when she was in trouble. She was a slippery thing; she could slip out of any punishment with a smile.

I looked into my parents' room next. They were sound asleep, and the noise machine my dad turned on at night was at full blast with ocean waves. I walked down the hall toward the back door, the floorboards creaking a bit. I heard the scratching again. Was Percy still outside? Come to think of it, I hadn't seen Macy brushing him before bed. She liked to brush him and sing songs to him at bedtime. Percy actually let her brush him, too. He hardly ever even let me pet him. It was as if he knew I liked dogs better. Even so, I didn't want him outside at night where he might be eaten by a raccoon.

I reached the living room and peered through the floor-to-ceiling glass window that looked out on our deck.

Scratch.

Scratch.

Scratch.

Leaves scattered across the deck in the breeze, but I didn't see Percy. I retreated down the hall to my room, and then I heard the sound again, like tiny nails on a chalkboard. Captain Sparkles must have heard too, because she slid off my bed and followed me as I returned to the window.

And then I saw the strangest thing on our deck.

A squirrel was standing on his two hind legs, like a prairie dog. I could see him through the glass. I inched closer, but the creature didn't scurry off, like a squirrel normally would when noticed by a person. He remained upright, with his front paws resting on his belly, staying perfectly still, maybe a foot away from the window. His bushy tail didn't even flick, but his eyes shifted back and forth every few seconds as if he were scanning the deck. I glanced at my canine companion. She had a nervous look in her eyes as she backed up slowly, slinking away from the squirrel on the other side of the glass even though she was safe and sound in the living room. I still needed to find Percy, but I didn't want to open the door and give the squirrel a chance to slip inside the house, so I used the dog door, pushing open the flap and sticking out my head.

"Percy, where are you? C'mon." I kept my eye on the small squirrel, who continued to stare into our living room. From my spot, I peered more closely at the creature since he was only a few feet away from me now. Beneath his paws was some sort of mark, like a black line across his belly.

Then I heard the sound of four paws zipping across the yard, rushing up the many steps and careening across the deck. "Percy!" I scooted back inside, then held the door flap open for him. He leapt through and let out the faintest little meow, a contrast to his yelping earlier in the day. He rubbed up against me, which he never did. As if he were trying to be nice.

Maybe it was time for a fresh start for Percy and me. I petted his sleek fur. "You've got a squirrel friend now," I said to him as he padded down the hall. Captain Sparkles followed him, nipping at his heels and batting his ears. He started to run, but it was more like a waddle. I laughed quietly at the dog's antics. Then she picked up speed and scampered after him as Percy turned the corner into Macy's room.

When I looked back at the living room, the strange, standing squirrel was no longer staring through the window. His head was tilted to the side, his ears were cocked, and he looked as if he were inspecting the dog door that our handyman, Danny, had installed that afternoon.

I'd never seen a squirrel take an interest in a dog door before.

The Collar in the Yard 3

I heard my dad wake up early the next morning. He had to leave town for a photo shoot at a drag race. He was an awesome photographer and snagged the best action shots of sports cars.

Since he was awake and packing, that meant I was awake too. I have super-bionic ears, so I wake up at just about any sound—the coyotes howling in the nearby woods, the teenagers down the street doing cannonballs in their pool, the neighbors' TV even, and they liked to watch TV shows on that network kids aren't supposed to watch.

My dad packed his suitcase as he talked to my mom in their bedroom. I listened from my bedroom.

"I told Danny I wanted a steel dog door," she said in her oh-so-very-ticked-off voice. "I wanted a steel dog door that locks at the bottom. Something safe and secure."

"Right, but that plastic door is fine," he said. My mom worried a lot. She was a grade A scaredy-cat, which was kind of ironic because she was a scientist, and she studied animal behavior. She could pick up a spider from my sister's floor with her bare hands and carry it outside, and she would laugh if a snake appeared on the deck, but she was always convinced someone was lurking right in our backyard. My mom got extra freaked out when my dad was about to leave town. It's not as if my dad was some big wrestling pro who'd slam a burglar to the ground.

"I'm going to get some wood and just board it up. Put a big X across the dog door."

"Steph, I love you, but that is totally ridiculous. Nothing is going to happen. I assure you. We live in the world's safest neighborhood."

"But you never know. This is how things happen. Someone leaves a door unlocked or a window open and then someone breaks inside. And you hear about burglars getting in through dog doors all the time."

"That stuff just doesn't happen here. That's why we live here, remember? That's why we left Springtown when Macy was born."

"Wes. We left Springtown because the neighbor's house was broken into."

My mom kind of had a point. A couple of burglars had broken into our neighbor's home in Springtown and stolen their TV, a laptop computer, and some jewelry. The jewelry part especially unnerved my mom. "It just seems so personal," my mom had said at the time. Then we moved here to Chatty Valley.

My dad said, "But don't forget, the neighbors didn't have a dog. Studies show burglars just don't break into homes with dogs. Captain will protect you."

"So do I ask for a two-by-four at the hardware store?"

Dad laughed. "Steph, if you're determined to board it up, please call Danny. We both know that, unless it involves a beaker or a microscope, you're about as handy as I am."

Then he came into my room to say goodbye to me. "How about a chocolate glazed donut when I return on Saturday?"

I nodded happily. "Is there anything better in the world than a chocolate donut?"

He pretended to think about it, then shook his head. "Not that I can think of," he said and gave me a hug. "The five-day donut countdown begins."

"Bye, Dad. And don't worry about Mom. Captain Sparkles and I will keep watch while you're gone."

A few minutes later, I heard my mom call Danny the handyman and ask him to swap out the plastic dog door for a steel one. But he must have been on his way out of town too, because she said to him, "All right, call me when you're back next week, and we'll take care of it then."

I hopped out of bed and walked to the living room. "Mom, you don't have to be scared when Dad is out of town. I'm here, and I'll protect us. I've been working on my karate kicks." I demonstrated a roundhouse kick that made me trip and fall on my butt. "Ow."

Here's the thing. I have CP, short for cerebral palsy. I was born with it. My mom says it's mild. I think it's annoying. I have to wear braces inside my shoes to help build up the weaker muscles in my feet, which are kind of flat. I hide the plastic braces with soccer socks folded over three times. If I didn't wear the braces, I'd have even more trouble trying to keep up with other kids at school. CP makes my brain send the wrong messages to my feet, like *trip, fall, run like a dork*. Which is another reason I don't like running—I'm not any good at it. With the braces, though, it just seems as if I have a slight limp. I've taken karate lessons and swimming exercises to keep my muscles strong and flexible because the doctor thinks that maybe I won't need the braces in a few years. Of course, getting rid of my braces didn't mean I'd be some speed demon or professional athlete. I just wanted to ditch the daily reminder that I'm not like everyone else, especially my lightning-fast sister who is four years younger.

My mom reached out and pulled me up. She put an arm around my shoulders. "Thanks, Ben. But it's my job to take care of you and your sister, and I plan to do just that."

When she scooted off to the kitchen to brew her morning coffee, I slipped outside to see if that strange squirrel was still lurking nearby. I held tight to the railing on the deck stairs, because I didn't want to slip and fall, especially since there were so many steps. When I reached the steep and craggy yard I was careful to step over fallen twigs and the dog's collection of old tennis balls. No one really cleaned up our yard or took care of it. It wasn't a grassy yard that needed to be mowed, but it sure looked like it could use a little maintenance. There were weeds growing in corners, jagged branches that had fallen off trees, and hedges that needed serious haircuts. Of course, if I alerted my parents, they'd make me do all of that, and I was kind of allergic to chores. Besides, hardly anyone used the yard. It was too steep to play in, and when we tossed tennis balls to Captain Sparkles we threw them from the deck, and she raced down the steps and into the yard to retrieve them.

I surveyed the yard, but I didn't see anything out of the ordinary.

I figured the strange squirrel was just that—a strange squirrel. But as I headed back up the stairs to get ready for school, I spotted something purple on the ground. I leaned down to check it out, and then I heard a rhythmic whacking.

"Twenty-two, twenty-three, twenty-four..."

It was Macy, and she was out on the deck, jumping rope.

"Hi Ben! Twenty-seven, twenty-eight. I'm going to set the record. Thirty."

"You skipped twenty-nine, Nutcase."

She shook her head and jumped some more. She was nutty. "I can count in my head and talk. Thirty-three, thirty-four..."

I ignored her and returned to the purple object. It looked liked a thick, frayed shoelace, and one end was sticking out from underneath a leaf. It was October and the air was turning crisp; leaves were starting to float down from trees. I pulled out the shoelace, but it wasn't a shoelace. It was a cat's collar. Was it Percy's? Had it fallen off last night when he was in the yard? Percy did have a new purple collar. But his nametag was circular, and this collar had a heart tag on it, tattered and faded, hanging from the middle. The heart made a slight tinkling sound as it hit the latch on the collar.

Macy must have heard the sound, because she called out from the deck.

"What did you find? A bell?"

"Nothing," I said, even though Macy was good at keeping secrets. But I wasn't ready to share this secret yet. I wanted to know more before I shared it with her.

"It doesn't sound like nothing. And it doesn't look like nothing." She'd tossed the jump rope aside and now stood at the top of the stairs, looking down at me.

"Well, it is nothing," I said, but I could feel my face reddening.

"Hey! That looks like Triple Latte's collar," Macy shouted excitedly. The next thing I knew, she was by my side, peering at the collar in my hand.

"Who's that?"

"He's my friend Caitlin's cat and he is so, so cute. He lives a few streets over, and he and Percy play together sometimes."

"What's his collar doing in our yard?"

"I think they have extra collars for him. He's always losing his collars because he chases other animals. The last time I saw him he was chasing a squirrel."

My spine straightened, and I tensed. "What did you just say?"

"He was chasing a squirrel. He's kind of in love with squirrels, Caitlin says."

"In love with them?"

"Oh, definitely. He loves to go after them. If one shows up at the window, he rushes over to it."

"Does Percy do that when he's there?"

"No. Percy just watches Triple Latte try to catch them."

"Does Triple Latte ever catch them?"

"It's pretty hard to catch a squirrel. But one time I saw Triple Latte chase a squirrel into a tree, and the next day there was a dead one on the road right near Caitlin's house," Macy said and wrinkled her nose. Then she frowned. "I think he was hit by a car."

I looked down at the collar. Triple Latte's name was engraved on the heart, with an address just a few blocks away. I wanted to ask what the squirrel looked like, but all squirrels kind of looked the same.

Unless they were standing weirdly.

It can't be the same squirrel, I told myself.

A squirrel was a squirrel was a squirrel.

"Ben! Macy! Time for school. Hurry up or you're going to be late."

I dropped the collar back to the ground. Squirrels, living or dead, were less fearsome than the look on Mom's face if you landed a tardy notice at school.

Scaredy-Cat 4

Remember that thing my mom said about having a plan while my dad was out of town? I learned that her plan involved staying up all night to keep watch over the dog door. I heard her make a pot of coffee at ten, then another one at midnight. She clacked away on her computer for another couple of hours, and the coffee must have been strong. I'd never heard the keys whizzing so fast. But the sounds stopped in the middle of the night, and the next time I woke up, it was courtesy of a bark.

"*Woof! Woof! Grr! Grrwoof! Woof!*"

I pulled off the covers, went to the back door, and found Captain Sparkles barking and staring at the plastic dog door, almost like she had X-ray vision.

"What's going on, girl?" I asked softly, kneeling down next to her. She barely noticed me. She was completely fixated on the door. And she wouldn't stop barking. "Do you need to go out?"

I figured I should let her out just in case she had to do her dog business. I opened the door, and she flung herself down the stairs like a missile.

The yard went silent, as if everything in it had frozen in place. I didn't hear anything for a minute, and I strained my ears, listening hard for Captain Sparkles. But there was no sound—no wind, no insects, no animal sounds.

I wanted to hear a noise. I wanted to know she was safe. Then all of a sudden I heard her, sprinting across the yard like a cheetah.

She raced up the steps, tail between her legs, ears pinned to her head, and eyes wide, like brown saucers. She skidded past me and pelted down the hall into my mom's room. I shut the back door, locked it, and went to check on her. She trembled in a corner, huddled near the closet door, ears still back.

"You okay, Captain?" I asked.

My mom stirred. "What's going on?"

"She was barking. She needed to go out."

My mom sat up straight in bed, suddenly alert. "What was she barking at? Was there a noise? Did someone get through the dog door?" My mom reached under her pillow and pulled out an aluminum flashlight the size of a baseball bat.

"The dog door is closed. The cover's still on it. It was just a noise in the yard, Mom. "

"What kind of noise?" she asked, throwing the covers off and tiptoeing to the window where she peeked around the edge of the blind. Her voice was higher, and she didn't sound just nervous. She sounded scared. I didn't want her to feel that way. I didn't want her to have to stay up all night worrying. But here she was, ready to fend off any attacks with her flashlight.

"Mom, no one's there. She probably just heard another dog. You know, down the street or something."

My mom tucked the flashlight back under her pillow. Only then did she notice Captain Sparkles. "Why is the dog shaking?"

"I don't know. Something scared her maybe?"

My mom raised an eyebrow in that way that only moms can raise eyebrows. "What would scare a dog?"

That was a very good question. Had the strange squirrel paid another late-night visit to our yard?

The other question was, where was Percy? My mom returned to bed, and I walked as quietly as I could, doing my best not to trip and fall, to Macy's room.

Percy sat contentedly at the foot of her bed. He didn't stare weirdly at my sister like he did with me sometimes. No, he just sat, a strange sort of satisfied gaze on his furry face. When I walked in, he looked at me and meowed. It was a quiet meow, not his usual braying one, nor the one that sounded like a cross between a beg and a whine for more canned cat food. He rose, stretched, padded closer to Macy, and lay back down, settling next to her. Then he placed his front right paw across her belly, as if he were claiming her, or maybe just reminding me that she was his favorite.

"I know you like her better," I whispered to the cat.

He looked away from me, but kept that paw firmly on my sister. As he turned I noticed his collar looked different. It didn't look new anymore. It looked tattered and frayed. It looked like Triple Latte's. I leaned in closer. As my fingers touched it, he turned back to me and opened his mouth. I half-expected him to start speaking, but everyone knows animals don't talk. Instead, he showed me the one fang he had, as if he were brandishing it as a weapon.

"Percy! You're so weird," I said to him. "No wonder no one likes you. You should be nicer to everyone."

He closed his mouth then and rested his head on my sleeping sister. He flipped over on his back, showing me his big, jiggly belly. From that pose, I could tell for sure he was wearing another cat's collar.

The collar of a cat who liked to chase squirrels into the street.

Squirrels that became roadkill.

5 Cat Messages

All I could think about the next day at school were Percy, Triple Latte's collar, and the strange standing squirrel. Were they connected? I wanted to ask my best friend Nathan, but he didn't know much about cats or squirrels. He had a bunny rabbit for a pet. Besides, Nathan's expertise lay in battles. That's why I made an epic trade with him at lunch—my strawberries for his garlic cheese bread.

"You know, strawberries make you stronger for battle," Nathan said, at his usual twenty-five-thousand-miles-per-hour speed. "Actually, all fruits and vegetables make you intense. That's what my mom told me. She told me broccoli, Brussels sprouts, cauliflower, apples, and strawberries make you tough, and muscular, and totally a better ninja warrior," he continued counting off each fruit or vegetable as he spoke.

"Dude, your mom is just trying to get you to eat your veggies."

"No, it's totally true. They do make you more awesome in battle."

"Did your mom also mention those are the foods you hate most?"

"No, it's true!" Nathan insisted. "My mom even showed me a story on the Internet. I can totally show it to you next time you come over. When are you coming over? When you come over we can pick out Halloween costumes on the Internet, even though I already know what I want to be. A ninja warrior!"

He jumped up from the table to show off a new ninja fight move, jutting out his right arm to smack an invisible enemy with his flat palm. "Take that!"

"Nathan Sampson!" A stern voice called out. "No battle moves on school grounds."

"Sorry, Ms. Bell." Nathan set school records for scoldings—he was yelled at easily seventeen or more times a day for talking too loud, jumping up in class, or fighting imaginary warriors. "I already ordered my costume. You have to come over and see the picture, and then we have to order yours. What do you want to be?"

We traded ideas for the rest of lunch until it was time for my least favorite class—gym. Our gym teacher was the happiest person in the world. He loved gym. He loved physical fitness. He loved running laps with us and cheering us on.

I loved none of the above.

"Now that you're fifth graders, you can all run the mile," he said in his chipper voice, then clapped a few times. "And I'm betting you can all do it in record time."

Seriously? He was seriously thinking we'd set records?

A bunch of kids clapped and cheered too. Inside, I groaned. I was a terrible runner. I was awful at everything in P.E. Plus, between my mom's computer clacking, the dog's late-night barking, and Percy's new neckwear, I was officially zonked.

Technically, I could get out of running the mile if I wanted. At the start of every school year, my mom and dad meet with the principal and my teacher to talk about my CP. The best part of those meetings is I can find out before all the other kids who my teacher will be. The

other part is my parents always tell the school I don't want any special treatment, because I don't. I want to be like other kids. I don't want to be singled out even if I have a disability.

Nathan and I started together, but he loves to run, because not only is he a ninja fiend, he's also an awesome athlete. He plays baseball and is one of the fastest players in his baseball league—the Thunder League. I didn't want to hold him back. He asked if it was cool if he took off ahead. He always asks me if it's cool. I always say yes.

I trudged around the field and used my alone time to think about Captain's endless barking, the eerie silence in our yard last night, and Percy's new collar. Why was Percy wearing Triple Latte's collar? Was the collar connected to the standing squirrel?

My mind churned with questions and, before I knew it, I finished the mile.

It took about fifteen minutes. Some of my classmates finished in ten minutes. Nathan finished in eight minutes. My mortal enemy, Rafael, finished in nine.

"Hey Ben. There's this thing called running. You put one foot in front of the other. Ever heard of it?" Rafael said when I left the field.

"Leave me alone, Rafael."

"Why does it take you so long to run?"

"I don't feel like talking about it."

"You're always the slowest one in gym," Rafael egged on. I wanted to point out that Rafael was the shortest kid in class. But I held back. My mom always tells me not to stoop to that level.

Instead, I went for a time-honored comeback. "Shut up, Rafael."

"Ooh, I'm scared." Rafael wiggled his fingers in the air, sneered at me, and walked away.

I wanted more than anything to run past him, but that would never happen. I was never going to be faster than him or anyone else. I was never going to outrun jerks. I gritted my teeth and looked down at the asphalt the whole way to my mom's car.

"I had the worst day at school." I slammed the car door behind me, because jerks like Rafael turned epic cheese-bread trades into nothing.

"My day was great!" Macy chirped, already perched in her car seat.

"I don't want to hear about it!"

"I had the best day because we ran the quarter-mile, and I was the fastest one in the whole first grade! I am super fast!"

"I was the last one to finish the mile," I blurted out and sunk down low in my seat.

It wasn't Macy's fault I was a dork. It wasn't her fault I'd never be good at sports. Still, I wished I were a scientist and could invent a pill to make me faster than my little sister. Or just the same speed. I'd take that. That was all I wanted anyway. To not be schooled by Nutcase every day in every thing.

I pulled my mom aside after we parked in our driveway. "Mom, am I always going to be slow? Am I always going to be a dork?"

"Ben," she said and put her hand on my arm. "You're not a dork. It's great that you can even run a mile. That's a serious accomplishment."

I gave her a hard look. "Mom. It's a mile. Anyone can do it."

"I'm not a good runner," she said. Then she lowered her voice in a whisper, like she was sharing a secret. "In fact, I hate running. I do everything I can to avoid it. So I bet you could beat me in a mile race."

I laughed a little. But then I stopped laughing when I saw Percy waiting for us on the front porch, next to the pumpkins we'd carved over the weekend. He never waited outside. Something small and furry hung from his mouth, and I clearly needed to conduct a clandestine inspection.

"Mom, you should see if there's any mail today," I suggested. "Doesn't your favorite science magazine arrive on Wednesdays?"

"You're right, Ben," she said with a smile and began the walk down our long driveway.

"Oh, look! It's my little darling cat waiting for us," Macy called out when she spotted Percy by the door, calling out to his favorite even with his mouth full. She skipped over to him, while I walked cautiously to the Siamese. I surveyed him from top to bottom, trying to figure out what green thing was hanging from his one fang-y tooth.

"Percy! You have Captain Sparkles's duck in your mouth," Macy declared and pointed to the cat. She turned back to me and laughed. "Look Ben! Percy's playing with dog toys!"

But I wasn't so sure it was playtime for Percy. He carried the head of the stuffed duck in his mouth, as if he'd ripped it off.

"Mommy will think this is so funny," Macy announced.

"Wait." I held out a hand. Then, in a soft voice, I said, "I think we should keep this a secret for now, Macy."

Her eyes lit up.

I'd just said the magic word. Macy loved secrets and prided herself on keeping them. Sometimes my dad took us out for ice cream and told us to keep it a secret from my mom. My mom didn't have anything against ice cream, but my dad got a thrill out of little secrets. Macy was a vault, locked and sealed, and only she had the key. One time, my dad took us to the ice-cream counter with my mom and Macy said, "This is so cool! I've never been here before!" She deserved an Academy Award for that performance.

She gave me a salute and mimed zipping her lips shut.

I didn't want to freak my mom out while Dad was out of town. At least, not until I truly knew what was up with our dastardly cat and the message he seemed to be sending with the severed duck's head.

Ruler of the Yard

Tip: If you are ever trying to get on a parent's good side, tell them you are going to bed early. Nothing—I repeat nothing in the whole wide world—makes them happier.

After last night, even my eyelids needed their own sleeping bag. I excused myself from the dinner table with a simple "I'm tired and I'm going to bed" announcement.

That sparked a big smile from my mom. "Be my guest."

I shuffled back to my bedroom, and Captain Sparkles trotted behind me. She spotted Percy curled up on Macy's beanbag, so she pounced and pinned him between her two front paws. I tensed because this was the moment when Percy usually hissed, then swatted a claw across her face. But Percy didn't even meow. He just lay there quietly and peacefully.

Only Percy was no pacifist, so I knew something was up.

But I was too tired to figure it out, so I crashed on my bed and fell asleep in my clothes. But at midnight I heard something that made me stir.

Flipping from my stomach to my back, I opened my eyes and strained to pick out the sound again. Like the wind, or a whistle. It was low, but it called out. There was a rhythm to it, a slow sort of whoosh, whoosh, whoosh.

I creaked down the hall, the floorboards squeaking as I walked. I heard the sound again coming through the dog door. The white plastic cover to the dog door lay in the middle of the living room, as if it had been blasted off, like wreckage from a battle.

I stopped in my tracks for a moment, hearing my mom's voice in my head: "Someone leaves a door unlocked or a window open and then someone breaks inside."

Was someone in our house? Or was some*thing* in our house? Some creature?

I jerked my head from side to side and spun around, but then tripped on my own awkward feet. I jammed my palms out to the floor and they broke my fall. But as I pushed myself back up, I knew no person had knocked the dog-door cover off with the force of a hurricane. I picked up the plastic cover and rested it against the back wall.

The sound came again. Whoosh, whoosh, whoosh.

I opened the back door and stepped out onto the deck.

I inched my way to the railing and scanned the yard below. A leaf blew by, skidding past me and toppling upside down, until it settled under the picnic table. A tree branch hanging over the deck swayed gently, but then I noticed there was no wind, so how could the branch be blowing?

I heard a faint rolling sound, looked down and saw one ratty tennis ball rolling across the deck, like it had a mind of its own. Then it went splat into the yard. When it hit the grass far below, a stick bounced up, way higher than sticks ordinarily bounce.

The stick levitated and hovered in the air, before it somersaulted back to the ground. A leaf raced across the deck, then another. One more joined in the fray, swirling around my feet before they all flew off the deck, like birds sailing across the night. The leaves swooped down to the yard, then fluttered up again, this time skating in tight circles. With each coil, more leaves joined, and soon hundreds of leaves looped around themselves, like a miniature leaf tornado in my yard.

But that wasn't the oddest part.

Because then Percy jumped down from a tree. He leapt off the branch and landed on all four legs. Like an elf, he was graceful and springy, which was a pretty impressive feat considering Percy was a total porker.

Then he stood upright, like the gray squirrel had. With his paw, Percy tapped the worn metal tag on his collar— on Triple Latte's collar—as if it were an amulet. He began to circle his front paws like he was the conductor of an orchestra. His furry paws blurred as he went faster. He stood majestically, all fifteen fat inches of him, as he worked his cat arms in front of his big belly. He was a wizard, a Jedi, a warrior commanding the troops. He was the leader of the yard, the ruler of the night, controlling the leaves, the ball, and the sticks.

He swung his arms feverishly, casting spells on the sticks, branches, and leaves. Soon, Percy had swept up the entire yard into his tornado. When the funnel grew as tall as the deck, brushing against my bare feet, Percy meowed. Just a regular cat meow. Nothing powerful or deep. Nothing that sounded like it came from a cat who suddenly had freaky weird powers.

"Meow."

The ground rumbled. The earth belched and, one by one, mounds of dirt cropped up in the yard. Like moles or groundhogs burrowing back up, the mounds rose until each was a foot tall. I shivered for a moment. I should have been nervous, but I was mesmerized. I'd never seen anything so unbelievably weird or spooky in my entire life.

I counted at least thirteen mounds in the yard. When they all reached the same height, shapes began to emerge through the dirt. I zeroed in on one of the mounds and watched as two small squirrel ears pushed up. Then the top of a squirrel's head, then a pair of dark beady eyes with tiny black slits for pupils, then a gray nose, then whiskers. The short, stubby front legs came next, then a furry stomach, then hind legs and a big, bushy tail.

This squirrel didn't quite look like your average squirrel. He was furry all right, but his gray fur shot up in all directions, like he'd stuck his paw in a socket and received a jolt of electricity. His eyes shone darkly, but they had a glazed, empty look, like the eyes of the squirrel on our deck last night had. Then jerkily, like a robot, the beady-eyed gray squirrel turned its head to Percy.

Percy gave him a quick nod. The gray squirrel turned its head back.

I finally peeled my eyes away from the gray one and saw a yard full of squirrels like him. They all stood on their back legs. They all had wild fur and the same glassy, empty eyes, which shifted back and forth. There was a big fat squirrel, and a tawny skinny squirrel, and a brown fluffy squirrel, and more. All the squirrels had one thing in common. Each belly was marked by a tire tread.

I spied the squirrel from the other night, hidden near the back of the pack. He stepped forward, robotic and clunky.

I remembered what Macy said—Percy's cat friend Triple Latte often chased squirrels into the street. And we all know that squirrels in streets can often wind up dead.

Roadkill.

My skin crawled with nerves, but I tried to bat them away. Because the beady-eyed gray squirrel might have been the one pursued by Triple Latte, then hit by a car.

I was willing to bet they'd all been hit by cars at one point.

Only they weren't really dead anymore.

They were zombies. Roadkill zombies.

7 The Purr Reappears

Percy waved an arm, and the thirteen undead squirrels marched to their leader. When they reached him, he dropped his arm and they stopped moving, standing at attention before him. Then he raised his other arm, spreading his claws wide. In unison, all thirteen zombies opened their mouths and took a deep, long breath. It was as if they were inhaling the yard and all the air in it. Then Percy retracted his claws and the zombie squirrels closed their mouths.

They were practicing, going through some sort of ritual, an exercise maybe. But what did it mean? What were they preparing to do with that collective inhale?

Percy moved his arm out to the side, like he was signaling to turn left while riding a bike. The crew vanished then, just as quickly as they'd appeared. Like a wave pulling back to the sea, every one of the squirrel zombies dropped down into its underground hole as if a trap door had opened, then closed. The leaves stopped swirling, the trees stopped shaking, and Percy walked on four legs again. He took his time, sniffed a bush here, smelled a piece of grass there. He stopped to stretch out his front legs before he pranced up the steps. Like he was a normal cat again, an average, ordinary feline out for a nighttime stroll and ready to come home.

I stared at him in disbelief. Was it all a dream? Should I shut my eyes tight like my mom tells me to do when I have nightmares? Once, I'd dreamed Captain Sparkles wandered across China looking for us. The next morning, I'd asked my mom how to stop those dreams. She'd told me to squeeze my eyes, yell "wake up" in my sleep, and yank myself out of the dream. Her technique sounded complicated, but if there was ever a time to try new tricks, this was it. I closed my eyes and shouted, "Wake up, Ben!"

Only it didn't sound like I said it in my sleep. Because I heard my own voice loud and clear.

My mom did too. She rustled in her bed, then walked down the hall. "Ben?"

Shoot! I had to get inside right away! I scooped up Percy, wondering if he had morphed into a zombie, too, to better command his squirrel minions. But his heart beat, his fur was warm, and he purred like a motorcycle starting. Percy never purred, not with me at least. Macy always claimed he purred so loud it shook her walls and she loved, loved, loved it. But he never purred with anyone else. Maybe this new purring Percy was an impostor. Maybe another cat had taken over his body.

I scrambled inside and slammed the door.

I spotted the dog-door cover where Percy had left it. But the dog door glared like evidence of my misdeeds—a boy playing outside late at night.

I grabbed the cover and shoved it back over the hole in the door, but I had a lot to explain to my mom. I wrapped the evidence—the cat, the dog door and me—into a one-size-fits-all cover-up. "I let Percy out. He...he had to pee."

My mom raised an eyebrow. "Percy had to pee outside? At night?"

"That's where pets go to the bathroom." I tried to act all cool, like duh, Mom.

She saw through me. "Percy uses the litter box. Or the planter. Or the flowers."

"When he's inside, Mom. And Percy does have outdoor privileges, so sometimes he just likes to go outside."

"I cannot believe we are having a conversation about the cat's bathroom preferences. But be that as it may, we

don't usually let him out at night just to pee. So tell the truth. Were you playing with the dog door again?"

Sweet! My mom gave me the perfect alibi.

"Actually, I was." I looked down at the floor and shuffled my feet. "And then Percy went through the door, and I know you don't like him outside at night because of the coyotes," I said, even though coyotes ought to cower before my cat. "I went on the deck and grabbed him before he ran down to the yard."

The same yard where Percy raised the dead.

"Shall we bring him to your sister's room then?"

"Great idea, Mom!"

I carried the roadkill zombie leader to Macy's room and deposited him on her bed. I wondered if he'd try to work his voodoo magic on Macy, if his newfound powers extended beyond the four-legged. Maybe he could make her stop talking so much. Percy curled up next to my sister's head, wrapping himself around her like a fat, furry snake, then meowed at us, sounding strangely sweet.

My mom tucked me in my bed and gave me a kiss on the forehead. "Stay in bed now, okay? You need your sleep."

"Yes, Mom."

But I didn't stay in my bed for long. I checked on our cat all through the night. He slept innocently enough, snuggled up against Macy. He didn't bare his fang at me. He didn't hiss at me. And he didn't dismember any more toys.

I checked on the dog door several times. It was securely in place. My yard was quiet too.

Too quiet. I walked past Percy one more time, and his tail twitched up and down on Macy's horse bedspread. It twitched like he was possessed. What had that collar done to him?

8 Payback

During my final round, at five in the morning, Percy had relocated to the dog's bed. He lounged on it, peaceful and calm, his eyes shut, his paws tucked neatly in front of him, his tail curled around his body. He'd never slept on the dog's bed before.

Why was he so content now that he'd raised his roadkill army? What was he planning?

Even though more questions bombarded my brain, I slipped back under my covers and managed to sleep for another hour.

Macy woke me up by galloping down the hallway, her short riding boots smacking loudly against the wood floor. "I'm riding Pomona today! I have my horse lesson today! I'm going to make Pomona run, run, run."

She trotted back the other way, and I thought about what I'd witnessed last night. Thirteen squirrels. Correction—thirteen *dead* squirrels. Wait, double correction—thirteen *undead* squirrels. Each one with a tire track down his belly. Each one bearing the evidence that it had died before its time, died in the way so many squirrels do—accidentally and under a car's wheel.

I shook my head. Was it all a vivid dream? I needed to conduct some recon, so I patted Captain Sparkles to wake her up. She jumped out of my bed, scampered down the hall, but stopped short when she saw Percy on her dog bed.

Uh oh.

She was going to tackle him, pin him down, let him know who was boss. But that's not what happened. Instead, Percy lazily opened an eye and gave her a quick, careless glance. Then he meowed a morning greeting and yawned, a big, fat, sleepy yawn, before he flipped onto his side and stretched out his whole body, raising his front legs casually above his head.

I was sure she'd pounce now. She'd wrestle him and maybe even nibble an ear, like she had tried to do that other night when I brought him in from the yard. But she just sniffed the bed cautiously, tilted her head to the side, then skirted around our suddenly cocky cat. Once she was a fair distance away from him, she wagged her tail. I let her outside and followed her to the top of the stairs. She sprinted down the steps and ran around the yard in circles, burning off a small dose of her morning energy.

Then she froze. The fur on her neck rose, then on her back, then on her tail. It was like she had an extra spine of fur. She let out a sad sort of worried whine as she dipped her nose to the grass and dirt. I ran down the steps—well, it was more like I clomped down the steps because of my CP. I was barefoot, so I was at my dorkiest, my flat feet hitting the steps like spatulas.

"What is it, girl?" I pushed the loose dirt and grass aside. Underneath the dirt was a hole about a foot and a half deep. There were twelve others just like it. I hadn't been dreaming last night at all. There were thirteen squirrels, living or unliving, in my backyard.

And they wanted something. I needed to find out what.

But I also needed to get to school. I rushed back up the long flight of stairs, switched out of pajamas and into jeans and a T-shirt, then carried my sneakers and braces into the kitchen. I jammed some toast in my mouth as I stuffed my feet into my braces, tugging at the Velcro straps on them.

Captain Sparkles had to stay in her crate during meals, so she watched me through the black bars of her kennel jail. I guess that was the point; she was something of a common criminal, because she stole our food from the table if we weren't looking.

As I tied my laces in between bites of toast, Percy strutted into the kitchen, greeting us with several noisy meows that translated into "feed me now," even though he'd already eaten. He paced around the crate, as if he were surveying it. Then he leapt on top of it. He never went near the crate. He never went near the dog, period. But he wasn't avoiding her anymore. He stretched out across her crate and reached his front paws over the edge. Then he stuck a paw through one of the slats and swatted the dog's snout.

"Percy! That was mean! Mom, Percy just hit Captain Sparkles!"

My mom popped into the kitchen. "What did you say?"

"The cat hit the dog. He was sitting on top of her crate and he smacked her."

But Percy had jumped off the crate and now appeared by my mom's side. He rubbed up against her leg and purred, like a lawnmower. Boy, that cat could switch from sour to sweet in a second.

"Ben, he's right here next to me."

"And my darling cat would never hit Captain Sparkles," Macy pointed out.

I stared hard at the cat. He looked satisfied. He looked pleased. He looked confident.

The tables were beginning to turn.

Research Project 9

All I could think about at school were those holes in the ground. Thirteen holes, thirteen holes, thirteen holes.

Each one covered with a thin layer of grass, dirt, bark and leaves. Each one home to a squirrel zombie. Each one controlled by my sister's very own chubby cat.

The funny thing was Percy had always been merely annoying. Once, when Percy knocked a soda onto the couch, my dad joked, "Percy, you've crossed the line from pet to pest."

That's all Percy had been. A pest. A trouble-maker. A naughty cat.

Now he was more. Something greater, something scarier.

As Ms. Livingston began our language arts lesson on creative storytelling, I fixed my eyes on the whiteboard like I was paying attention. But questions raced through me. What did Percy want? What powers did zombie squirrels have? Should I tell my mom?

Hi, Mom. I have something to tell you. There are thirteen squirrel zombies hanging out in our backyard. Pretty wild, huh? Yeah, you were right to be all freaked out about things going bump in the night.

I thought back to how she slept with the heavy flashlight under her pillow, how she made herself extra coffee to keep watch, how she worried. My mom was already terrified that someone or something lurked outside. If she knew that thirteen undead squirrels really and truly prowled our yard, she'd totally freak out, pack us up and make us live in an igloo in Antarctica, thinking that'd be the safest place on the planet.

I didn't want to live in Antarctica, and I didn't want my mom to be scared all the time. Besides, maybe there was nothing to be scared of. Maybe squirrel zombies were like regular squirrels—mostly harmless.

For now, I'd keep the zombies to myself.

Which meant one thing and one thing only.

I had to figure out what they wanted.

The only problem was I didn't know the first thing about squirrel zombies. I didn't know the first thing about any kind of zombies.

But it was time for library, and we had to work on our first-ever book report. Technically, this wasn't my first book report. My mom had made me practice writing them over the summer, which was so not the way I wanted to spend my summer vacation, but she was nutty strict about homework and stuff. Even when my friends came over after school, she made us do homework first before we played computer games or Monopoly or staged battles in the driveway.

"For your book reports, please choose a book you are excited about and interested in. You can choose a story or a non-fiction book if there is a particular topic you want to learn more about," Ms. Livingston instructed as she led our class into the library.

That was it! Books. There was a book for everything. There had to be a book on zombies.

"I want a book where there are lots of battles and fights," Nathan said as we walked past the shelves with the fancy award-winning books. "And all the guys go pow-

pow-pow and then they go kaboom and bam and whack!" Nathan finished with a flourish, bouncing down to one knee, then back up again.

"Yeah, that'd be cool," I said, even though I knew that wasn't the type of book I'd check out.

"And definitely one with lots of weapons and swords and all sorts of cool stuff and the characters go boom, bam, crunch, kill!" Nathan pretended to chop off a bad guy's head.

"Nathan Sampson," Ms. Livingston said, "You don't need to reenact the Battle of Gettysburg in the library. But since you are so keen on it, perhaps you can do a book report on it."

"I'm sorry, Ms. Livingston. I'll go find a book now." Nathan raced to the faraway shelves.

I walked up to the librarian's desk. "I know what I want to do my book report on."

"And what would that be?" Mr. Fong, the school librarian, asked me as he looked up from the computer. He knew everything about every subject ever written. He spoke in a low, kind of creaky voice and had gnarled hands that looked like skinny old tree trunks.

"Zombies."

"You like scary stories," he said with a sparkle in his eyes.

"I don't want a story."

"You're not looking for *Goosebumps*? Maybe a little *Bunnicula*? Something to give you the heebie-jeebies before you go to sleep?" He wiggled his fingers at me.

"Who'd want the heebie-jeebies?"

"Halloween is coming up in three weeks. A lot of kids like spooky stories this time of year."

I wanted to tell him I didn't need a book for a spooky story. I'd just open my back door.

"I want a non-fiction book on zombies. One of those complete guides. Like they have for archaeology and the solar system and stuff like that."

Mr. Fong leaned in to whisper, his rickety voice lower than usual. "They don't have those kind of zombie books *here*," he said, emphasizing the last word. Here.

I whispered back. "Where do they have them?"

"You're talking real zombies, right?"

I nodded.

He narrowed his eyes at me. "Of the mammalian kind?"

Another nod.

He leaned in closer this time, pointing a grizzled old finger at me. "They won't let me carry those kind of books here. And I've tried, believe you me. I want our students armed for everything." He glanced around to see if anyone was looking, then pulled a piece of scrap paper from his desk drawer and scratched out a couple words on it. "I happen to know the Halloween Hideout carries them." He paused, lowered his voice even more. Good thing I had rocking hearing. "But you have to know how to ask for them."

"How do you ask for them?"

He folded the paper in half, then in half again. "Take this. But do not read it on the school grounds. Understand?"

I took the paper, thrust it into my pocket, and nodded. "Have you ever met a zombie?"

He scoffed, then waved a gnarled hand at me, maybe even a hand that had once fought off a zombie. "What do you take me for? Someone who fell off the bookshelf yesterday? Now, go pick out a nice, safe book for your book report, and after school you go get yourself the book that matters. I suspect you'll need it sooner rather than later. Time is of the essence when you're dealing with the undead."

The question was, how much time?

10
A
Witch's Wart

I contemplated how to convince my mom to take me to the Halloween Hideout as I walked to my last class of the day, Chorus. Should I ask her to drop me off, or to go with me? Could I plant the idea in her head that she should go enjoy a cup of coffee at the nearby coffee shop, so I could slip into the Halloween Hideout? I ran through my options as I headed up the risers in the music room. Since I'm tall, I sat on the highest bench, and Nathan sat in the middle. As I walked past Nathan, I tripped and smacked my chin on the metal edge of the riser.

"Ouch," I said, quietly, because I didn't want everyone to look at me. But I was tangled up, and one of my sneakers with my stupid dumb brace in it was stuck between the risers. I tugged, and I pulled, and I yanked, but still my chin hurt, my foot refused to budge, and I felt like the biggest dork in the whole entire universe. I felt a hand on my sneaker and Nathan said, "Here buddy, just twist it a bit." I moved my foot slightly and my shoe came unstuck.

"Thanks." When I sat down, everyone was staring at me. "I'm fine," I mumbled. I wished they'd turn their heads to Mr. Plesser and start singing "We are the World," the song we were practicing for the fifth-grade assembly.

"It's like you have a witch's wart on your chin!"

Rafael. That bleeping Rafael.

I touched my chin. Great. I had a giant goose egg from the fall. Now I'd be sporting a big bump on my chin for the next week.

"You could be a witch for Halloween! Let's just put hair on it!"

"Rafael, be quiet," Mr. Plesser said.

Nathan jumped up from his seat and marched down the risers to Rafael. "You already look like a witch and you don't even have a bump on your chin from falling, so take that, witch-boy!"

Uh-oh. Nathan was going to get himself a detention in three, two, one...

"Nathan Sampson and Rafael Marcado. That kind of behavior is rude and uncalled for, and it is not in the spirit of Chatty Valley Elementary. Both of you be here tomorrow morning a full hour before school starts to reshelve the books in the music library. Now kindly take your seats."

Mr. Plesser walked up to me and said softly, "That's a nasty bruise. Why don't you go to the nurse's office and get some ice?"

"Doesn't hurt." I shook my head.

"You really should put ice on it."

"I'm fine."

Then we sang about harmony and peace while I pictured Rafael walking into school with his underwear on his head. Now I felt harmonious and peaceful. After chorus ended, Nathan had all but forgotten about his detention. "I'm going to make my mom take me to Halloween Hideout today before baseball practice! I gotta find extra cool totally awesome stuff for my ninja costume," he said as we walked to the parking lot, but before I could even say, "Can I come?" he scooted into his car and was off.

I decided to try my luck with my mom.

"Hi, Mom. Can we go to the Halloween Hideout?" I slid into the backseat of her car.

"We're taking Macy horseback riding today, don't you remember?"

Oh, of course. I should have remembered Macy's schedule. I should have tattooed every detail of Nutcase's daily to-do list on my forehead.

"I'm going to ride on Pomona, and today I'm going to make him fly, and then I'll win a blue ribbon," Macy sang.

The thing was, she probably *would* win a blue ribbon. Then a gold, then a silver, then a purple. Then she'd get a trophy the size of a pony, and it would come to life and waltz with her while she sang the National Anthem at the World Series, and everyone would clap and cheer because she was the youngest, and the cutest, and the most talented kid on the whole planet.

My mom eyed me through the rear-view mirror. "Ben, what happened to your chin?"

"I tripped in chorus and got my foot stuck, and that stupid Rafael made fun of me."

She reached a hand back and patted my leg for a second. "That's not a nice thing for him to do. And that doesn't sound like fun at all, getting a bruise like that."

"It wasn't fun," I said as she pulled away from the school. "And it still hurts."

"Did you put ice on it?"

"No, I didn't want to. I'm sick of being the dork who's always tripping and falling and needing ice for his head or his chin or his eye. And something like this will happen to me next week when I fall again because I always fall! I wish I didn't have CP!" I banged my fist against the back of the passenger seat.

"You're not supposed to hit the seat," Macy called out. "Mommy, Ben hit the seat. Mommy!"

"Macy, be quiet," my mom said as the car slowed at the stoplight. She turned back to me again. "I'm sorry, sweetie. I'm sorry you feel that way. I know it must be totally frustrating sometimes."

Then an idea popped into my head. A brilliant idea. Because, let's face it, sometimes brilliant ideas come to you when you're ten years old. "Mom, since I had such a sucky day, do you think I could go to the Halloween Hideout instead of Macy's horseback riding lesson? Because Nathan is going to the Halloween Hideout, so if you just call his mom right now and ask her then I bet I could go with her and Nathan. It would really make me feel better after falling in chorus today."

She picked up her phone and within seconds I was on my way to the Halloween Hideout.

Never underestimate the benefit of a good chin bruise.

11 Wingman

Nathan's mom had to take a phone call from her oh-so-annoying boss (that's what she said as the phone rang), so she sent us into the Halloween Hideout by ourselves.

I hoped her oh-so-annoying boss would be particularly annoying today and annoy her for a very long time. As the door swung shut behind us, I pulled Mr. Fong's note from my pocket and read it for the first time. It was detailed, it was strange, and it would involve a "performance" of sorts to gain admission to the secret backroom where the zombie books were kept.

Plus, I'd have to escape Nathan for several minutes to conduct this mission. Sure, Nathan would be distracted by ninja gear, but would that buy me enough time to snag a zombie book?

"What are you going to look for first?" I asked Nathan as a cackling laugh echoed throughout the store, followed by a spooky scream sound effect. We walked past the scary baby display, where a gray psycho baby gnawed on a foot. The green baby next to him rolled its head all the way around on its neck.

"Nunchucks! I want nunchucks and swords! And I want a belt that has all sorts of pockets and pouches that I can hide all my secret weapons in because I'm going to battle all the bad guys on Halloween. Every last one of them." Nathan stopped in the middle of the aisle and air-punched an imaginary bad guy. Behind him a mummy in a net rolled back and forth across the floor.

"Watch out for the mummy. He's trying to trip you," I joked.

"I'll battle mummies too and skeletons and monsters and vampires..."

He went on and on, rattling off every single bad guy, and that's when it hit me. I didn't have to do this alone! I was best friends with a fighting machine. Nathan watched kung-fu movies, studied jiu-jitsu, and knew every single thing about wrestling choke holds and ninja moves. He would be the perfect teammate in my battle against the zombies. He could be my wingman.

"Nathan, I have to tell you something, if you promise to keep it a secret and not tell anyone in the whole world. Not even your mom and not even Fluffy," I added. Fluffy was Nathan's pet bunny.

"Dude! I never tell secrets. You know that. Warrior's code."

I glanced around. We were surrounded on one side by a wall of masks—blood-dripping creature heads, freaky dudes with rolling eyeballs, and pale ghost faces. Across from us was a graveyard scene, with tombstones covered in spider webs and rickety fence posts draped in "Keep Out" signs. Beneath the tombstones, bodies popped up from underground and cried out in low, rumbling moans.

Then a robotic black cat prowled across a headstone.

I jumped. The cat was just a toy, but I'd been learning that cats weren't always what they seemed, including my own cat, who now had some strange power to control squirrels. I pulled Nathan aside. "Okay, I know this is going to sound totally crazy and whacked. But..."

I told Nathan about the dog door, the standing squirrel on the deck, Captain's barking, and the thirteen squirrel zombies with their tire-tracked bellies. Nathan's eyes grew bigger and wider with every detail until they finally looked like they would pop out of his head.

"We need machetes and battle axes and we will fight, fight, fight! This is what all my battle training has been for. The squirrel zombie invasion."

"There's just one small problem. We don't actually know how to fight squirrel zombies."

"Like this." He wielded a make-believe sword like he was going for the throat.

"I don't know. Squirrels are sneaky. They're fast, and they're hard to catch. I don't know if we can fight them like that. But, if we go to the back of the store we might learn how to fight them," I said, because that's what Mr. Fong's note told me to do.

We walked past Snow Whites, bumblebees, and mermaid costumes. I glanced around to make sure no one was following us. I didn't want to be caught in the baby costume section. Who wore these things anyway? Who would want to be a red ladybug?

When we reached the entrance to a storeroom area, I knew we'd arrived at the right spot. A pair of black curtains hung down. A blacklight filtered through them, like the light inside a haunted house. I strained my ears, but I heard nothing except the sound of wind and eerie graveyards wafting through the store itself.

Gulp.

I was about to summon a zombie hunter.

I followed the directions on my note and hooted softly three times.

Nathan looked at me like I was crazy. Maybe I was.

But then we heard the sound of scuffling feet, in old clunky boots, dragging across the floor.

Double Dose

12

"**W**ho seeks entry into my lair?" a low voice asked. I tried not to quiver or run or shake.

"We have need of your midnight knowledge," I said, repeating the words on the notepaper.

"Demonstrate," the voice commanded in a growl.

I wondered how he'd see me, but I was too nervous to ask. I crouched down, low to the ground. It wasn't easy for me, squat-walking like this. Nathan would have been much better, but he hadn't seen the squirrel zombies. So I imitated the beasts, taking several slow, plodding steps.

Nathan laughed, but I shook my head and held a finger to my lips. He shut up. I clunked a few more steps, then repeated the words on the note. "They do not eat acorns. They do not run across tree branches. They do not climb trees."

"Ah, very well then!" the voice said, turning cheerful, chipper, and British.

The guy behind the curtain emerged, holding it open as he beamed at us. He wasn't old or creepy or scary. He wore jeans and a button-down shirt. He looked about my dad's age, sported a big bald spot, and wore a friendly smile on his face. "Nigel Marchbanks at your service. Do come in! I can help you with your squirrel zombie problem. Would you like some tea?"

"Uh, no thanks."

"Do you have Super Green Energy Tea?" Nathan asked. "You know, the bubbly kind in the black and green bottle with the big ram on the front."

"I'm afraid I don't. Shortbread cookie instead?"

Nathan and I shrugged and grabbed some chairs.

The back room was like a small warehouse. We were surrounded by boxes of Halloween costumes on long metal shelves. A stereo system on one wall piped out the spooky sound effects. Next to the stereo rested a CD that said Monsters, Vampires and other Ghoulish Noises. Stacked up in a corner were body parts—plastic legs and arms, as well as heads, hands, and feet. It was as if the curtain had been pulled back on the Halloween displays and we could see them in the light. They weren't so scary in the warehouse.

Nigel sat down at a rickety wooden desk with lots of small cubbyholes and slots for books and pens. The desk had a roll-top cover. He pulled it open, revealing a plate of cookies. He offered us some. I shook my head. Talking to him was one thing. Taking food was another. Nathan reached a hand out, and I shot him a quick look, so he pulled back.

Nigel popped a cookie into his mouth, ate it, and began talking.

We learned that Nigel had battled a family of zombie raccoons in Connecticut, fought off reanimated cats all the way in Ireland, and defeated a whole battalion of chipmunk zombies in Montana. Surely, he could help with the infestation of squirrel zombies my cat had summoned.

"It's not easy, mates," he warned us and took a small book from the back pocket of his jeans. It was thin and looked like a pamphlet. "It's all in here," he said, tapping the pamphlet. I read the title: *A Brief History of Animal Zombies and the Battles They Have Waged*. He stuffed it in his pocket. "Any zombie with four legs is much more dangerous than a zombie with two legs."

Animal zombies were worse than human zombies? I rolled my eyes in dread. "Great. Why is that?"

"You see, lads, it makes perfect sense. Think about it— animals are creatures of instinct. They have to fight for survival. They have to prowl for food. But humans? We get lazy, we watch too much TV, we eat too many Doritos. We drive fancy cars and talk on cell phones, but we know nothing about how to survive. Animals, though, that's all they do. They're hard-wired to survive. They run on instinct. They're naturally better fighters than we are. All those traits carry over when animals become zombies. It follows that animal zombies are faster, more agile, and more clever than people zombies."

I held up a hand. "Are there people zombies too?"

Nigel laughed deeply and shook his head. "No, boys. You have nothing to fear from two-legged zombies. People zombies are extinct. They died out when convenience stores became popular. They haven't been seen since. We zombie hunters believe it's because they ate too much processed food, and that killed them off rather quickly. Darwinism is alive and well in the zombie world. Human zombies were too much like humans, so they died out. And, just as animal zombies assume the traits of their living animal counterparts, human zombies also took on the traits of human beings. Humans no longer had to fight for their survival. They didn't have to hunt food or protect their family in the wild from predators. The human zombies followed suit. They became caricatures of themselves—clunking around aimlessly, flailing across the land. But animal zombies," he said, then paused, as if he were paying his respects for animal zombies, "were and are stronger, faster, tougher, and smarter. So they rose up, and over time more species of animals have become zombies."

My head was spinning. "How exactly does an animal become a zombie?"

"Animal zombies must have a commander. They must have a leader. Animals naturally want to live in a hierarchy, and because most animal clans have a leader, most zombie animal clans do as well. Animals, and animal zombies, respond well to order, leadership, and structure."

My eyes bugged out. "The zombies at my house totally have a leader, and it's my cat! Well, my crazy sister's cat."

I explained about Percy, how he'd summoned the zombies last night, how he stood there, tiny yet triumphant, and commanded them to rise from the ground.

Something didn't add up, though. "But Percy's not dead. He's still alive. I don't really understand how he can be the leader, especially since he's, obviously, not even a squirrel. How can he summon them and how can he be the leader?"

Wonder, with a touch of surprise too, filled Nigel's eyes as he leaned forward in his desk chair. "That is unusual. Oftentimes, a living cat can discover the secret to commanding undead members of his very same species. Back in Ireland, when a clan of cat zombies rose up in the countryside, it was because a barnyard cat had raised several feral cats from the dead. For cat zombies to appear, they must always have a living cat leader."

"But Percy didn't create a cat zombie army," I said, thinking that a cat zombie army would be a bit sad. Cats were pets. I didn't want them to become scary creatures of the night.

Nigel nodded, and rubbed his hands together, as if he were searching for an answer. "That's what's so odd about your situation. Your cat crossed species in his zombie army creation. It's such a rare occurrence, one I've only seen a few times. Is he one of those squirrel-chasing cats?"

I shook my head, then told him about Triple Latte and his predilection for squirrels.

"Ah, perhaps this Triple Latte fellow is his partner. You say Percy's wearing his collar. He's likely wearing it to channel some of Triple Latte's interactions with squirrels."

Nathan had a confused look on his face. He raised his hand as if we were in class. "What does that mean?"

"If this Triple Latte is a squirrel chaser, and has, through his chasing, played a role in the demise of a squirrel, then Triple Latte would be able to summon a squirrel zombie, but only—"

I interrupted Nigel. "But Percy can only do it if Percy is wearing something of Triple Latte's, right?"

"I was actually going to say something else, but yes, that's vital too. For a living animal to summon zombies, he requires the presence of an actual physical object from either the dead animal he's raising or from the living animal that last interacted with the dead animal."

I snapped my fingers. "So Triple Latte must have chased that standing squirrel back when the squirrel was alive and caused him to be hit by a car, so Percy needed Triple Latte's collar as some sort of conduit to zombie-summoning powers?"

"Indeed," Nigel said with a nod. "Zombies can't just be created out of thin air. And most animals never become zombies because there are too many necessary conditions for summoning them. The physical object is needed, which your cat found through his squirrel-chasing friend. A living animal leader can also call zombies forth under two additional and very specific conditions."

"What are the two conditions?"

"The first is need. The living cat must have a need for a zombie army. When this need arises, if and only if he has access, he can reach out to the undead squirrels."

"The cat has a need? Like they need to eat or need to sleep?"

"I'm actually talking about a deeper need. An emotional need."

"All that cat's emotional needs get met by Ben's crazy sister. She's all 'I love you, Percy. Have some tea, Percy,'" Nathan said, imitating Macy. I covered my mouth to keep from laughing.

"That is good to hear." Nigel leaned forward in his creaky wooden chair. "Because you should give all your pets love and affection. As humans who live with animals, it is both our responsibility and our pleasure to treat animals with love, and also to train them."

"Percy's not trainable. Even my mom says cats can't be trained. And she's a scientist. She studies all kinds of animal behavior, so she knows."

"But cats can be loved."

"So what's the other condition?" I asked.

Nigel went on. "Access, my boys, is key. There are two conditions for a dead animal revival. The first is a need. The second is sort of akin to a portal. An entry point, if you will. Something man-made that wasn't there—"

"—that wasn't there before," I finished his sentence. I knew what the man-made portal was. "A dog door."

That dang dog door.

Big Breath

13

Nigel turned back to his desk and rooted through some papers. He pulled out a handful of photographs.

"Yes, lads. A dog door is often the very mechanism a wily cat needs," he said, handing Nathan and me a half-dozen pictures. I flipped through them—photos of all sorts of dog doors. Plastic ones, steel ones, sliding ones. "Those are some of the animal zombie portals I've photographed over the years. You see, pet owners install dog doors thinking it makes life easier for themselves and for the dog. But oftentimes, a problem cat simply seizes the opportunity and uses the dog door for his very own nefarious purposes. A dog door then becomes a portal for undead animal entry. That barnyard cat in the Ireland countryside used a dog door, too."

My mom was right when she wanted to rip that dog door off and board it up. I should have glued it closed with Super Glue.

Then I thought about the last words Nigel said. A portal for undead animal entry.

Entry could only mean one thing.

"They're going to come into my house," I said heavily. It wasn't a question anymore. The invasion was a certainty.

"That is their goal, Ben."

"And what will they do when they get inside?"

Nigel looked up at the ceiling, then rubbed his chin. "You know, boys. This reminds me. Chatty Valley had a squirrel zombie infestation in the late summer."

"Late summer? Like just a month ago?"

"Yes. Rumor is the zombies weren't handled properly. Even so, it's all here in black and white," he said, tapping his back pocket where he'd tucked the pamphlet. "That's my extra copy. Just landed back on my desk a few days ago. Co-worker had borrowed it for a good mate of his."

"There are rules for handling zombies?" I asked.

"Absolutely. There are techniques for battling them and for disposing of them properly to ensure they won't rise again. I have a hunch your squirrel zombies might be a double dose, a term for a recurring pack of zombies. It's been known to happen with cat, squirrel, chipmunk and duck zombies in particular, because people often think they're easy to battle. They're cute, they're small, and they seem innocent. Many people don't take any of these animal zombies seriously. Most people get careless when battling these type of zombies. They pick the wrong weapons, underestimate the creatures. When that happens, the animal zombies will disappear for a few weeks, maybe a few months. But they'll come back, and they'll be stronger, and when they're stronger, you have your work cut out for you in fighting them. They'll often assume even more traits of their living counterparts. That may mean that your squirrel zombies start assuming the traits of their leader—of your very own cat."

"Great. Just great. So not only do I have a zombie squirrel problem, I also have a double helping. And to top it off, these squirrel zombies are going to start acting like my own crazy cat, who's a total troublemaker?"

"It seems you might be bearing the brunt of someone else's improper zombie disposal. But never fear; as long as you follow the proper procedures, they won't change the behavior of other animals."

"Excuse me? Change the behavior?"

"Dear boy, animal zombies want nothing more than to feed off the energy of living animals, and then transform their behavior."

"Into what?"

"Animal zombies need other mammals to behave like them in order to survive. Just as movies had us believe that human zombies needed brains, we now know that animal zombies need the energy of living animals, and when they take that energy, the living animals assume the traits of the zombies. Raccoon zombies who feed off another animal's energy may cause their targets to become nocturnal. Bunny zombies may make another creature nervous all the time. Duck zombies might make another animal waddle."

"Whoa. That is crazy," I said, as I shook my head. I had figured animal zombies would bite you and turn you into a zombie. But this was...weirder. "How does it happen? How do they change your behavior?"

"The zombies breathe in the energy of other mammals, except the leader, of course. The living leader, having raised the zombies, is immune to their transformative powers, which grow stronger each night. But all other living animals are vulnerable to zombies and to their breath-sucking power, especially if they go anywhere near the zombie burrows."

"Oh no." I dropped my face into my hands. I had let Captain Sparkles out this morning, and she'd sniffed the zombie holes in the ground. I had to get home. I had to see her.

"This is all part of their hope for an eventual Zombie Animal Apocalypse," Nigel added.

"What is that?" I asked as I picked up on a pair of voices from deep inside the store. It sounded as if someone was being interrogated.

"The day when animal zombies rule the animal kingdom. When they've infected all other mammals and made them act like their zombie-kind."

"Is that really going to happen?" Nathan asked.

"I strive every day to keep it from happening, sport. As long as there are zombie hunters, we can save the world from the Zombie Apocalypse. That is what they want, these zombie squirrels in your yard. They want to inhale the energy of other animals in order to change the behavior of those other animals. To recreate other animals in their image. Being above ground strengthens them, and by the third night they may have gained enough strength to enter your house and cause all the animals there to behave like squirrels."

I had spotted that lone squirrel zombie a few nights ago. But, as far as I knew, Percy didn't summon the army until last night. So I had two more nights. Tonight and tomorrow night.

"So how do we stop them? Chop their little heads off?" I asked, feeling instantly queasy. Even though the zombies were dangerous, they were still little squirrels. They might not be house pets, but I didn't want to chop any creature's head off, not even my sister's Barbies. (Wait, scratch that. I would definitely chop Barbie heads off, if Macy had any Barbies.) But before Nigel could answer, I had an idea! The collar! I could just take Triple Latte's collar off Percy and we'd be fine! The collar was how Percy was able to channel the zombies in the first place. All I had to do was cut his connection and the zombies would probably wither and die.

Well, die again.

"I know what to do! I know how to defeat them!" I shouted happily. Then I heard another sound—the distinctive clicking of heels.

Nigel gave me a curious look. But before he could say anything or ask anything, a loud voice tore through the store.

"Nathan James Samuel Sampson! You have three seconds!"

Nathan scrambled instantly, racing out of the back room.

"Thank you, Nigel." I started to leave.

"Wait," he said quickly. "Take this book and study it!" He thrust the pamphlet at me and I stuffed it into my jeans pocket. "You'll need reinforcements. Bring your friend there. That'll help while you prepare the—"

"Ben Fox! Three, two..."

"—weapons."

I didn't hear the word he said before *weapons*. But I had no choice. I had to go or I'd face something even scarier than a pack of zombies. This was Nathan's mom we were talking about.

14 Cat Burrito

And Nathan's mom wasn't happy.

"Nathan and Ben. I expected more from you. You're fifth graders. You should know better than to go off in the back room of a store and disappear for so long. A Halloween store at that! I trusted you to just look around. Instead, what do you do?"

She gave us that look. That look parents give kids when they are not happy with them in any way, shape, or form. "I thought you were gone. I thought you left the store. I looked through that whole store twice and couldn't find you. And then when I asked the manager, who I might add looks like a member of the living dead himself"—Nathan and I exchanged a glance and a snicker, because she had it all wrong—"he tells me you're off in the back room of all places. And I heard you seconds ago, yukking it up with Mr. I-Seem-So-Safe-Because-I-Have-An-English-Accent!" She stopped to take a deep breath. Her voice softened. "I was worried. You have no idea how fast my heart was beating when I couldn't find you. I felt horrible. Because it would have been my own fault. I let you go in there by yourselves so I could take a stupid work call. Please tell me you won't do that ever again."

"We won't, Mom. Don't cry." Nathan wrapped his arms around his mom. She hugged him tightly, then pulled me into the hug.

"I'm sorry I worried you, Mrs. Sampson," I said. "Are you going to tell my mom?"

"Of course I'm going to tell your mom."

Just my luck. But my mom was the least of my worries, because Captain Sparkles didn't greet me at the door when I returned home. I peered around the corner, hoping she was in her crate and my mom had forgotten to let her out.

But the crate was empty.

I called out to her. She didn't run or bound or race through the house. Instead, she sashayed, then arched her back. My dog, my sturdy, tennis ball-chasing, tail-wagging dog, was starting to act like a cat. I scratched my head because this was weirder that I expected. I thought she'd start acting like a squirrel—hoarding nuts and scurrying across tree branches. But feline behavior?

Oh, it was a topsy-turvy world.

"Captain," I whispered. "What's happening to you?"

She rubbed her side against my leg. I petted her, and she circled my legs a few times, then my mom berated me for taking off in the store. After I apologized twenty million times, I tracked down Percy. He wasn't sunning himself in his usual spot on Macy's pillow, where he liked to catch late-afternoon rays through her window. I found him taunting the dog again, lounging like he was a swimsuit model across the dog's bed. Boy, that cat made my blood boil.

I shook my finger at him and narrowed my eyes. "I've figured you out, Percy. I know what makes you tick, and I know how to stop it."

I kneeled down and reached for his collar. But he brandished a claw at me, in a lazy, devil-may-care way.

This was going to be harder than I thought. I tried again, darting my hands toward his neck as quickly as I could. "You're not going to win, Percy," I said.

The other paw came at me. But he was gentle this time, strangely subtle. He laid his paw across my wrist, and I looked down at it before I could grab hold of his collar. As I did, he showed me his claws, just barely grazing my skin with them in warning. He hadn't drawn blood, but it was clear he would if I came any closer. He didn't want me touching his power source. I was more sure than ever that all his zombie leadership skills lay in that purple collar. I thought about the time he'd had a tooth infection a year ago and my parents had to give him antibiotics. My mom practically suited up in full astronaut gear as my dad wrapped him in a towel, like a cat burrito, then pinned him down as my mom jammed a pill down his throat. I'd have to do the same, even though there was only one of me. I raced down the hall to grab a towel from the bathroom, but as I started to wrap him up in it, he wriggled away, rushing off to Macy's room.

He was a squirrelly one, and clearly he was going to fight me if I tried to take off his collar. But there was one person he would never fight. The one he loved.

I headed straight for the deck to find my secret weapon of a sister.

Carrot Soup

15

"Three-hundred thirty-four, three-hundred thirty-five," Macy counted out as she swung the jump rope over her head, skipping it perfectly as it hit the deck, each and every time.

"Macy, remember that secret we talked about yesterday?"

She nodded happily and kept counting. "About the duck toy."

"Yes. Listen, I'm super worried that Percy might get toys and stuff stuck in his collar if he keeps playing with them."

She gave me a strange look. "Three-hundred forty-eight. Why would he get toys stuck in his collar?"

"I think that collar he has on is too tight. I think we need to take it off."

She dropped the jump rope and motioned for me to follow her inside. She raced to her room and slammed the door. "Let's help him right away. I don't want anything to happen to him."

She climbed up on her bed and started to fumble around with Percy's collar. But the one thing Macy wasn't good at was taking watches on and off, or putting on the clasps on necklaces and stuff. I knew she wasn't going to be able to do it. That was the point.

"Macy, we need to cut it off him," I said. Then I whispered to her. "I think something's wrong with this collar. I think it'll always go back to being too tight, and we just can't take chances."

She hopped off her bed, then grabbed a pair of scissors from her desk and walked carefully back to the cat. Percy eyed her cautiously. But he didn't seem bothered when she slowly slid one blade under the collar and one blade over it, then sliced through.

Triple Latte's collar made a jangly sound as it fell on Macy's bedcovers. "Whew. He's okay now," I said and breathed a huge sigh of relief. "Now, hide that collar somewhere. Mom will be mad if she knows we cut it off, but the point was to save Percy, not to preserve a silly collar."

"I would have been so worried about him," Macy said, as she stuffed the collar inside her toy chest, then gave Percy a big, cuddly hug. I left Macy and Percy to their snugglefest and returned to the dog.

She'd found a cat toy, a pom-pom ball with a bell in it and was batting it across the floor with her front paws. I stayed near her as I worked on my homework and my mom worked on her latest research report on her computer. When Captain Sparkles shifted from the pom-pom ball to using Percy's scratching post to sharpen her claws, it was clear the collar strategy had failed. I had thought she'd resume all her dog-like behavior the second we cut the collar, almost like cutting off power to a house. Wasn't that cutting off Percy's power supply to the zombies?

I figured I better take a quick peek at the zombie pamphlet to make sure I hadn't missed something. I slid the pamphlet into the middle of my math workbook so my mom wouldn't see it and opened to the first page of *A Brief History of Animal Zombie Warfare*.

Greetings, fellow zombie hunters! And welcome to the cause! Read on for all the details on how to battle and handle every breed of animal zombie known to man. This manual will prepare you for nearly every challenge you might face, with detailed strategies and tactics. I urge you to read the primary guidelines on the raising of animal zombies, for information is power, and to effectively fight any zombie, we must understand them.

But Nigel had already explained how Percy created his army—through Triple Latte's collar. So I scanned the guidelines, skimming over the details about how a parrot had once led a battalion of wild turkey zombies, as well as the rare instance of a skunk leading a rat army. That image was sure to give me nightmares. I was ready to skip the rest of the guidelines when I came across the final page.

A side note on animal zombies. In order to raise an undead army, the living leader must touch something that belongs to a dead creature, and that gives him the initial connection—like turning a key in a car's ignition. Cats, for instance, often rely on collars for this spark, since a collar is usually the only wardrobe item a cat can ever truly call his own. Bear in mind, a cat only needs the collar to raise the army. Once he has summoned his soldiers, the full command powers are now vested in the living cat, and the zombies—whether cat zombies or an inter-species army—will do his bidding. The collar then becomes purely ceremonial and decorative.

I read it another time, then another, wishing I was reading it wrong, wishing the words were out of order. My heart felt heavy and my head felt stupid. How could I have thought it would be so easy to vanquish zombies? Nigel, himself, had warned not to take shortcuts. Cutting off a collar was the ultimate shortcut, and it clearly hadn't worked. I tried to remember what Nigel had said about weapons. He was trying to tell me what kind of weapons I'd need to battle the squirrel zombies, but I hadn't listened because Nathan's mom was calling us then, and I had been too fixated on the collar anyway.

I was mad at myself. But I didn't have time to be mad. I needed facts. My mom was still typing on her computer a few feet away.

"Hey, Mom, do you think I can go back to the Halloween Hideout? I forgot something I wanted to get for my costume."

She raised her eyebrows. "What's your costume?"

"Um," I said, stumbling on my words. I hadn't thought this through. I didn't even know what I wanted to be for Halloween.

"I don't think you were Halloween shopping when you were there. You were goofing off. So the answer is 'no.' You can't go to the Halloween Hideout again today."

"But, Mom. I really need this."

She gave me a look that said not to push it. "Ben, I'm disappointed in your behavior and in the fact that you seem a little sneaky right now. So you know what? I think you should spend the next hour playing nicely with your sister. That will be your grounding. You have to play whatever she wants to play."

"Mom!"

"Ben," she said, coolly and calmly.

"I need to finish my homework," I grumbled, pointing to the newspaper next to her at the table. "My current-events assignment. I need the newspaper, please."

She handed me the front section. "Here you go. Go to your room. Sit at your desk and finish your work. Then play nicely with Macy. Anything she wants."

"Yes, Mom." I shut up and trudged down the hall, thinking of other options for fighting zombies.

I looked over the newspaper to hunt for a topic. I found a couple stories that didn't bore me to pieces, circled the headlines, and tucked the paper in my homework folder to show my mom later. Then, I began to formulate a plan for tonight and tomorrow. I would need Nathan for tomorrow, so I called him on Face Chatter.

"We need to convince our moms to let you sleep over tomorrow night," I started, sharing the details of the plan. I'd handle the pests tonight, I figured. But I'd need Nathan tomorrow on the third night.

"You think they'll go for it after we got in trouble today?"

"I hope so. My mom's still mad at me, but tomorrow is a Friday night. Is your mom still mad at you?"

"She took away my ninja toys, and all my weapons, and all my video games for a week."

"Oh, she's mad for sure," I said.

"What did your mom do?"

"My mom likes creative punishments. So, for my punishment, I have to play with my sister. Anything she wants."

"Ouch."

"Anyway, I'll talk to my mom about the sleepover tonight. I'll find a way, because I'm not going to battle those zombies alone."

I hung up as Macy swept into my room. "Mommy said you're going to play with me, and I want to play with the horses. Come on! Let's braid their manes."

The next thing I knew, I was on my sister's pink pony carpet, braiding the hair of all her plastic horses and serving them carrot soup in blue and pink teacups.

"Carrot soup is their favorite!" Macy declared. "Oh, look! This horse wants another!" She handed me a gray and white horse, and I fed him carrot soup, which turned into apple stew, which became a block of sugar with cinnamon frosting, just the way Polka Dot the Horse liked it.

"Maybe he'd like some hot chocolate," my mom said as she walked into Macy's room with two mugs of hot chocolate.

Score!

Hot chocolate meant one thing and one thing only. I was getting back on my mom's good side by playing nicely with my sister. The nicer I was to everyone, the more likely my mom would be to say yes to a sleepover.

"I figured with your horseback riding, Macy, and your fall today, Ben, you could both use a treat." She handed a cup to Macy and one to me. She wasn't mad anymore about the Halloween Hideout. The sleepover request was going to be easy!

"Oh, this is just so, so delicious," Macy said.

"Actually, this is your best ever, Mom," I said. I didn't want to be outdone by Nutcase. I stood up to give her a hug. "I love you, Mom."

"Well, aren't you a little sweetheart?"

"It's true. You're the best mom in the whole world."

"And you, my suddenly delightful young man, are still required to be nice to your sister. So you two keep playing while I make spaghetti for dinner."

"Can I help you set the table, Mom?"

She reached out and placed a palm on my forehead. "Yes, you definitely feel hot. I had a feeling you were running a fever," she said, and winked at me.

"I just want to help my mom. You sit down and relax, and I'll make dinner."

She raised her eyebrows at me and said, "Just play with Macy. Thanks."

Percy wanted to join us too. Because he pranced into Macy's room, and for the first time, I realized his eyes looked a little glassy, a little empty. Just like the zombies. Uh-oh. I had a feeling he'd be growing even more powerful, while Captain Sparkles would turn ever more cat-like.

16 Naked Cat

After a few bites of my mom's spaghetti—which I said tasted so good she should open an Italian restaurant—I hit her up for the big one.

I cleared my throat and placed my hands together. "Mom, I was thinking...since tomorrow is Friday night, and since Dad isn't home until Saturday, and since I fell in music class, and since I've been playing really well with Macy, maybe I could have Nathan sleep over tomorrow night."

Was there any way she could say no to such a brilliantly worded request?

"Ben, you've only been playing nice with Macy for the last hour since you got in trouble."

"And you're usually mean to me," Macy said.

"I'm not usually mean to you." This was going downhill quickly.

"You kind of are," Macy said.

"I'm not mean to you. Mom, am I mean to her?"

"I don't think you're *mean* to her," she started, but you could tell she was being diplomatic. "It's just that sometimes you're dismissive. But still, I don't think one hour of being nice means you can have a sleepover, Ben."

"We'll be good, I promise. We'll go to bed by eight-thirty, even eight if you want. And we'll play quietly, and we'll clean up our mess."

"Ben."

"We'll even make our own peanut-butter sandwiches for dinner. Please, Mom! Please, please, please, please, please." If I had to keep asking for the rest of the night, that's what I would do. "Please let me have a sleepover. I promise. I've been good all week, and I let Captain Sparkles out at night, and I took care of Percy when he went outside the other night, and I've been working hard on training the dog to be nice to the cat." The last part wasn't true. I hadn't worked on cat-dog relations since Percy had turned into Señor Psycho. But if she thought I was nice to the untrainable cat, that might tip the scales in my favor.

"I'm just not sure it's such a good idea so soon. Maybe another night."

I wanted to tell her tomorrow night was the only night that mattered. Tomorrow night could be the start of the Zombie Apocalypse, and I needed Nathan by my side to fight. Maybe it was time to come clean. Maybe it was time to enlist my mom in the battle against the undead animal clan. She'd want to save the dog from the crazy effect of the zombie squirrels. Plus, she was an animal behavior expert, and that would come in handy since Percy was doing some serious cross-species voodoo shenanigans.

As I considered the right words to say, Percy strolled into the kitchen. He lifted his chin, sniffed the air, then jumped on the table, announcing his arrival with a hearty meow that stretched on for several syllables. He landed right next to the meatballs and dipped his nostrils near the food.

"Oh! My little darling wants to join us for dinner!"

"Percy! Off the table now," my mom said sternly. But he padded over to her, stepping over the bread, then rubbed his head against my mom's shoulder. "What a strange cat you are," she said as she picked him up and plunked him down on the floor. She regarded him for another second or two, then said to us, "Have you guys seen Percy's collar? He's naked right now."

Both Macy and I cracked up at that word. "Naked cat! That's funny!"

My mom laughed, too, then asked again. "Did you see it anywhere? Maybe out in the yard?"

"Mom, you can't find anything in that yard," Macy said. "It's a total mess."

I gave my sister an approving nod. She was indeed excellent at the storage of secrets.

"True, very true. I guess I'll have to pick up a new collar for him tomorrow," my mom said, shaking her head. "It's always something with that cat, isn't it? He's such a troublemaker."

Percy was a troublemaker and he'd gone too far. I needed to tell my mom. I took a deep breath. "Mom, I know why Percy's being so strange these days."

She narrowed her eyebrows at me curiously, then waited for me to say more.

I gulped. It was now or never.

"Well," I began, drawing out my words because I was nervous, "I'm pretty sure it's because Percy has learned how to command an army of squirrel zombies, and he's got thirteen of them ready in the backyard to try to invade our house to make Captain Sparkles act like a cat all the time."

There was a long pause.

Then my mom burst out laughing. She laughed so hard she snorted, smacked the table with her palm, and spit out some of the iced tea she was drinking. "That is a good one, Ben. A very funny joke."

"It's not a joke, Mom." My face felt hot. I had confessed the truth, and she was laughing at me.

"Ben," she said. "Squirrel zombies? Really?"

"Yes. Really."

"But does that even make sense? He's a cat. Wouldn't he be more likely to raise an army of, say, cat zombies?"

"Mom! I'm serious."

"As am I. I would think a cat would rely on the same species to invade our house."

"It's even more dangerous when animals raise armies of other creature zombies," I said, as my voice rose. I must have sounded ridiculous, but I wanted to convince her. "I saw them! They're going to come in our house through the dog door and breathe in all the dog's energy so she acts like a cat twenty-four-seven. That's why she's acting weird today—playing with cat toys and scratching her claws."

She stopped laughing and shot me a serious look. "Ben, I said it was a good joke. But you have to know when to end a joke. I don't appreciate you playing on my concerns about the dog door. You know how I feel about it. So let's just move on. Besides, I think it's pretty safe to say that I know a thing or two about animals, and I feel confident there is no such thing as a zombie squirrel, nor a cat who can raise zombie armies. And if Captain Sparkles is acting like a cat, well, it's just because she's a young, playful dog having fun."

Stopping the zombies fell on my shoulders.

Because it didn't look like Nathan could join me either. I called him after dinner and told him my mom had nixed the sleepover idea.

"So how on earth am I supposed to battle the zombies without you?"

"Dude. A warrior always has a backup plan. And I have one."

"You do?" I said, perking up.

"It's totally easy. Nigel said you'd need me because I'm fast. Well, who else do you know who's really, super, incredibly fast?"

A Brief History of Animal Zombie Warfare

17

Macy. Macy as my partner? Macy as a fellow zombie battler?

It didn't fit. She was Macy. Happy, bubbly, crazy, high-pitched, skipping, singing, horse-loving, cat-coddling Macy. She'd probably try to serenade the zombies to death.

But, on the other hand, she had already helped. She'd discovered Triple Latte's collar in the yard, she'd shared all the details of our cat's friendship with him, she'd spotted the duck in Percy's mouth, and she was the only one who could get close enough to our cat, as she'd demonstrated earlier when she snipped off his collar. That might be a needed battle skill.

Still, there had to be another way. But I didn't have much time to find it. The one thing I needed for sure was to understand the enemy. After my mom tucked me into bed, I grabbed a copy of Calvin and Hobbes and stuck Nigel's pamphlet in between the pages so my mom couldn't see it if she came in. I began reading *A Brief History of Animal Zombies and the Battles They Have Waged*.

The chipmunk, at first glance, looks cute and cuddly. After all, it's a forest animal, and it fits in your palm. Some chipmunks have even been domesticated and kept as pets. And let us not forget how the movies try to convince us of the sweet innocence of this creature. But when risen from the dead, a chipmunk can be fearsome. Though only weighing in at a mere three ounces in most cases, the chipmunk zombie should be avoided if possible. They move nearly as fast as living chipmunks. That's why I was shocked when I first came across a chipmunk zombie; I had expected the zombie one sees in films—clunky, plodding, and dumb.

But this is not an accurate representation. These fictions are handed down from filmmakers and writers, but have no bearing on reality. Because the real story of a chipmunk zombie is extreme speed. Chipmunk zombies will chase dogs, cats, hamsters, guinea pigs, even horses. If they come close enough, the zombies will gnaw at their feet in hordes in an attempt to topple them, steal their energy, and make them behave in a chipmunkian manner.

How, then, does a zombie hunter fight them off?

As one must with any form of animal zombie: you locate its weakness. And you do this by studying the animal and understanding the animal. Every animal has a weakness— sometimes it's food, sometimes it's a habit, sometimes it's one of the basic building blocks of life. When you know their weakness, they will usually succumb to it.

You must do your homework and carefully observe any animal zombie you need to battle. That is precisely how I uncovered the secret to battling chipmunks several years ago when I encountered a rather sizable platoon of undead chipmunks in Laurel, Montana. I had researched their habits, their likes and their dislikes. It is a well-known fact that chipmunks live in elaborate and well—constructed tunnels, and they are quite fastidious creatures. They make sure to keep the sleeping quarters in their burrows completely free of shells, nuts, and other waste products.

I knew then that cleanliness, and the all—consuming need for it, would likely be the downfall of the zombie chipmunks, for they too had also constructed elaborate burrows, mirroring their living counterparts. I brought a large bag of peanut shells, walnut shells, almond shells, pecan shells, and even pistachio shells with me and poured them into the zombie chipmunk burrows. Immediately, the zombie chipmunks began cleaning, and I continued filling their burrows with more shells. That made them frantic, and they cleaned faster and faster just to keep up. Remember, chipmunk zombies are speedy, and if you can get them going, their speed will get the better of them. They cleaned faster, and still faster, like spinning tops moving so quickly they became blurs. And they spun so fast they soon popped!

I then swept up the usual assortment of remains and disposed of them according to Zombie Hunter Protocols, since I am certified in Hazardous, Dangerous, and Extremely Toxic Zombie Small Animal Removal. (Helpful Hint: A Ziploc bag will work just fine for amateur zombie hunters.)

Do remember that, except in the rare occasions where a release is possible, a pop is always the goal with animal zombie warfare. The only way to properly eradicate an animal zombie is via the all-important pop, which you can most effectively achieve by fighting back against the animal zombie via its weakness.

So zombies popped. That was how an animal zombie met its demise. But what sort of pop? Like a messy explosion? Or more like a magical poof, a now-you-see-it-now-you-don't kind of thing? Did they pop like balloons? Or bombs? What kind of mess did they make? A nasty, slimy mess? And what exactly was a release? What sort of "rare occasion" created a release?

I needed more information.

But as I started the section on the Raccoon Wars of 1999, I heard a loud yawn. I snapped the Calvin and Hobbes shut, hiding the pamphlet inside. My mom walked down the hall.

"You should really go to bed, Mom," I called out.

She poked her head into my room. "And fall asleep before you? Hah."

I wanted to point out that I'd be up tonight and tomorrow, keeping watch, keeping order in the animal kingdom.

Fortunately, I knew how to induce extreme sleepiness in my mom.

"Hey, Mom! You know that current-events presentation I have to do for social studies? Well, I found a couple stories in the paper, but I'm not sure if they're good ideas or not. Can you look at them for me and let me know what you think?"

"Sure."

I gave a big (fake) yawn and pointed tiredly to my desk. I pulled my blanket tighter under my chin as if I were ready to fall asleep any second. "It's in my homework folder." I rubbed my eyes for good measure.

She took the newspaper and said she'd read the articles shortly. Perfect. Nothing put her to bed faster than reading the news.

I listened to her brush her teeth and wash her face. The tinkling of Captain's collar told me the dog was on her way down the hall. She wandered into my room and wagged her tail twice. She was acting like a dog again! This was great! Then, she spotted my open T-shirt drawer and hopped into it. It was a classic Percy move. I'd seen him sleep in many a dresser drawer. My heart sank.

"Hey girl," I whispered. "You'll be back to normal soon."

I stayed still and quiet in my bedroom, waiting for my mom to fall asleep too. I heard her open the paper, then a few seconds later she was snoring.

The newspaper trick worked like a charm.

I returned to the raccoon saga.

When I was a lad, after my family moved to the States, a neighborhood raccoon appeared on our front porch late at night to finish the leftover kibble in our dog's food bowl. He'd stand on his back legs and dip both paws into the bowl, bringing the dry food up to his mouth, using his paws like human hands.

This knowledge came in handy years later when I was called upon to eradicate an entire family of raccoon zombies that had encroached on the country home of a kindly couple in Somers, Connecticut, targeting the prize parakeets and toucans inside their home. The raccoon infestation began in their nearby fields, but over the course of a mere two nights, the bandit—like animals advanced on the home. I received the call of alarm that final evening and hopped into the trusty green Triumph I'd had imported. Now, I was a skilled zombie hunter at that point, already having fought off chipmunks, rabbits, and gophers. So when I arrived at their country home I had a keen sense of what the raccoons' plan of attack would be.

I discerned their intention immediately when they held up their front paws in the universal sign of "put up your dukes" as I pulled into the long gravel driveway. Yes, they wanted to battle me with fisticuffs, like a bunch of schoolyard punks.

I was ready. When I hopped out of my vehicular transport, they welcomed me as one of their own. Why, you ask? Because I was already wearing my black bandit mask across my eyes, and I had a litre of soda inside my jacket. They must have thought I was behaving like them, so they put their paws down immediately, their way of inviting me into the fold. Next, I offered them a drink. One by one, using their agile paws, they each took a swig of the bubbly, sugary beverage. What happened next? Why, the very thing that happens when anyone drinks too much soda. Only it happens much, much faster with zombie-fied raccoons. They all popped.

Pop. Pop. Pop.

Right there. On the driveway. They popped in the air, and then they were gone.

I scooped up the raccoon remains and disposed of them properly. The old couple thanked me and offered to take me out for fish and chips. I declined, for I had just received notice that a pair of squirrel zombies was on the loose in a neighboring county. Off I went, stopping only at the local fruit and vegetable stand to procure two slightly rotting pumpkins, because it is a little-known fact that squirrels adore pumpkins. The squirrels had already marched up to the front porch of a rather large and stately old manor. They were rattling against the door, banging their matted gray fur against the firm wood and attempting to take deep breaths by the doorjamb, as if they could begin their breath-sucking, behavior-changing inhalation under the door itself. Still, time was of the essence, as it always is with the undead. I flicked open my Swiss Army knife, cut off the tops, and quickly carved out the insides of the pumpkins. Then I deposited the orange fruits on the porch and stepped back to the nearby bushes to watch surreptitiously. Immediately, each of the undead squirrels hopped into a pumpkin, unable to resist the taste of the fruit's innards. This was my easiest battle yet. I re-emerged from the bushes, plunked the pumpkin tops back on, then shook each pumpkin and voila!

Zombie squirrels, begone.

I put the pamphlet down for a moment. Halloween was coming. We'd carved pumpkins last weekend. They were on our front porch. This would be easy. I'd grab them and shake up the squirrels! The only catch was the whole cross-species thing Nigel had mentioned. Hmmm. I returned to the book to hunt down any additional information on cross-species animal zombies.

The next few months were quiet ones, and the rash of infestations ceased. I spent the time honing my skills and studying living animals in the wild, to prepare for whatever might come next. What came next proved to be the most dangerous battle yet. I would be dealing with the most powerful strain of animal zombie known to man— a cross-species army of roadkill skunk zombies, led by a living bunny rabbit—

I turned the page, eager to learn how to defeat the bunny-led roadkill zombies. But nothing was there. Just a bunch of ripped-out remains of pages in the middle of the book. I flipped to the back. The only thing left was a chapter on duck zombies.

"Where's the bleeping section?" I flipped through the whole pamphlet again in case I missed it. But the section was gone. The cross-species roadkill pages had been torn out. My mind flicked back to the chat with Nigel earlier today when he'd said, "That's my extra copy. Just landed back on my desk a few days ago. Co-worker had borrowed it for a good mate of his."

Hmm. I wondered if maybe that good mate had torn out the pages for some reason.

But whatever had happened to the section didn't matter now.

I'd have to figure this out on my own. I'd have to fight off those fearsome roadkill zombies as Nigel had done. I walked as quietly as I could to the front door and unlocked it. I grabbed both pumpkins, one in each arm, and shut the front door with my elbow. I brought the pumpkins to the back door and left them there, ready to be filled with zombie squirrels shortly. I returned to my room and gave Captain Sparkles a pat on the head and checked my clock. Ten PM. Two more hours until the squirrel zombies woke up. I set my alarm for 11:55 and drifted off into a fitful sleep, as an entire flock of grizzled duck zombies with half-rotten beaks descended on my house. When I woke up, I was grateful, momentarily, that the duck zombies were just a dream.

The Battle Begins 18

J ust before midnight, I headed for the kitchen and took the last swig of milk, straight from the carton. I'd need my energy and my strength to keep watch for the rest of the night. I returned the empty milk carton to the fridge, then walked to the back door. The pumpkins were in place, but the dog door cover was blown off again, blasted into the middle of the living room, but still whole. Percy had moved fast tonight. He'd mobilized his troops in mere seconds. When I opened the back door, I saw that one by one, squirrel by squirrel, the zombies were already marching up the steps onto my deck. The gray one trekked up first, then bowed to Percy, who stood waiting in the center of the deck, like a host at a restaurant. Next was the big fat squirrel, then the tawny skinny one, then the brown fluffy squirrel. Percy nodded to each one and held out his right arm as if he were pointing. They walked past Percy in their strange rhythmic path to the edge of the deck. Then I saw where they were headed. In the corner, my dog cowered on her side.

She was supposed to be in my room! She was supposed to be asleep! She must have escaped when Percy escaped. I bet she heard him sneak outside when I drank the milk. At least she still behaved like a dog at times, and she was obviously such a good security dog that she'd wanted to check things out and protect us. But I had to protect her from turning full cat.

"No!"

I yanked the door open so far it clanged against the side of the house. I rushed to Captain Sparkles just as the gray squirrel zombie leaned his crusty, matted furry face to her.

"Move it, you creepy squirrel," I said, slamming an elbow in his fur. The squirrel tilted his head to the side, opened his mouth, and let out a strange sound that was almost like a meow.

Whoa.

The zombie squirrels were starting to sound like their leader.

I grabbed my dog's collar and pulled her up in record time, keeping her as far away from the gray squirrel as possible. But he didn't stop. He followed me as I dragged Captain Sparkles to the door and pushed her back into the house. The squirrel zombie matched me step for step. I jammed another elbow into him, but he kept coming. I grabbed a pumpkin and turned it on its side in the doorway, hoping Nigel's trick would work. The squirrel marched into the pumpkin. I was shaking inside from nerves, but I had to stay strong for my dog, so I followed Nigel's instructions. I dropped the top back on and rattled the pumpkin. When I removed the top, I expected to find a "popped" squirrel zombie.

Instead, I found a squirrel zombie reaching one paw over the side of the pumpkin. He pulled himself out, like a cat slinking out of a box. These were no ordinary squirrel zombies. They were feline-esque, and I didn't know the secret to beating cat zombies yet.

I went for a temporary solution as I stood in the doorway. With Captain Sparkles safely inside the house, I grabbed Percy by the neck like a momma cat does, since he was still collar-free, and jerked him away from his pack. He hissed and scratched like a wild thing, but I held on tight. I wasn't going to let him wriggle away like he had earlier in the day. I turned back into my house, but I tripped on the entryway and dropped Percy. He tried to escape and rejoin his army, but I lunged after him and grabbed his tail. He spun around, and yowled at me, grappling at my hand with his sharp claws, but I held on tight to his tail like it was a lifeline. Even while he hissed and spat at me, then jammed his sharp little teeth into my hand.

"Ow!"

But his bite was all I needed to get a better angle on him, so I wrapped my arms around his chubby belly and gripped tightly. Then I shut the door and jammed the dog door cover back on.

"You have crossed the line from pet to pain," I said to him. Then, I grabbed the dog's collar and carefully walked her across the living room, so she'd be safe with me, while holding onto the cat around his middle. I refused to let either one out of my sight with those zombies nearby. I took Percy to Macy's room, dropped him onto her bed, and shut the door so he couldn't escape. I brought Captain Sparkles to my room, and she curled up next to a stuffed animal dog I had won at the fair last summer by guessing the carnival guy's age. I checked on the cat again to make sure he wasn't hurting Macy. Instead, he was lying next to her and doing that thing cats do when they play the piano with their paws. One minute he was mean, the next minute he was loving everything.

I returned to the back door and locked it while the squirrel zombies wandered aimlessly across the deck, looking for their missing cat leader.

I thought about waking up my mom. I'd march her right up to the deck and show her that zombie squirrels were real and their behavior was super freaky, because they were acting completely like cats. The leader was obviously setting the tone. But she'd just call animal control and dispose of them improperly. Then they'd come back in a quadruple dose. Plus, I didn't want to leave my post for any reason. I kept my eyes on the undead squirrels as they circled the deck, like lions in a zoo, back and forth. But after a few orbits, they slowed down. They stumbled and bumped into each other, helpless without their living cat leader. Then they retreated down the steps and into their zombie burrows.

I returned to my room to find Captain Sparkles washing her face by licking her front paws. I dropped my head into my hands. Was she going to play the piano on the bed next?

There was only one thing for me to do. Enlist a fellow soldier in the battle. Besides, that fellow soldier had already proven herself many times over. I just needed to make it official.

I petted Captain once more, then shut my door, keeping her safe in my room for the rest of the night. I stationed myself against the dog door. I could hold the zombies off tonight, but I couldn't cut any corners in the final standoff tomorrow.

They were transforming my dog, and that meant war.

19 Lieutenant Macy

"**M**acy, wake up," I whispered.

My sister shifted under her horse covers.

"Macy, time to get up."

"Why are you waking me up, Ben?"

"Macy, remember the thing with Percy's collar? And the duck toy in his mouth? And what I said to Mom at dinner last night?"

She nodded.

"Well, Mom didn't believe me, and that's why we still have to keep it secret from her. And I know you are the best in the world at keeping secrets."

She sat up straight as a ruler, a good student eager for the teacher's instructions.

"I need your help with something important. A huge secret. It's going to sound crazy, but Percy is mad at us, so he created an army of squirrel zombies, and tonight they're going to break into the house, steal our energy, and make Captain Sparkles act like a cat all the time."

"I like cats."

"I know, but do you really want the dog to sleep twenty-two hours a day and to use a litter box? Or do you want to throw tennis balls to her and take her to the beach?"

"Okay, fine. I like the beach."

"Good. Because I have a plan, and you and I have to defeat them. But Mom can't know because if she knows she'll do things her way, she'll do them the 'scientist' way," I said, sketching air quotes with my fingers. "But she doesn't understand this kind of animal behavior."

Macy laughed. "Mommy always thinks she knows best. Because she's a scientist."

"But this time she doesn't. Because she hasn't studied and researched zombie animals, and I have. So if we tell Mommy, everything will get messed up. So I really need you to help and to keep this secret." I lingered on the last word, her favorite word, like it was bait.

Macy bait.

"A big secret?"

"So big no one can know. Not your friends. And not your stuffies and not your horsies. This will be the biggest secret ever. And you're the only one I know who can keep secrets like this."

She nodded solemnly. She didn't ask for proof. She didn't ask questions. "Sure! What do I have to do?"

That was one of the great things about being six. You were usually up for anything. Macy liked to run errands, to fold laundry, to play sports, to play with horses, and now, to hunt zombies.

"We have to start now before Mom wakes up."

Macy jumped out of bed, an eager lieutenant.

"Follow me to the kitchen."

I opened the fridge and explained my plan. I'd figured it out while I was falling asleep and thinking of the way the squirrel zombie had meowed and slunk around and how Captain was doing the same. I had a hunch we should battle them as if they were cat zombies. "I remembered we're out of milk. You know how Mom is about milk. We always have to have milk in the house. So she'll want to buy more milk today. And if we only need one thing, she'll just go to the corner store by herself. But, if we're out of lots of food she'll have to go shopping, and she always waits until after school and takes us with her. That's the key to the plan—the grocery store." I grabbed Macy by the shoulder to emphasize my point. "And since we need to go to the grocery store to beat the squirrel zombies, we have to make sure Mom needs to go shopping."

"Why do we have to go shopping to beat the zombies?" Macy asked as I began yanking slices of bread out of the bag.

"Supplies. We'll need supplies to make our weapons. We'll get those supplies at the grocery store."

I handed Macy the loose slices of bread, then I stuffed a few pieces back in the bag and put the bag back in the fridge. "Run outside and toss this bread into the trash can."

"Why do I have to?"

"You like being fast, right, Macy?"

She nodded.

"Faster than anyone else in school and faster than me?"

She nodded again.

"That's why. You're fast. I'm not. I will be the lookout and let you know if I hear Mom wake up. Plus, if you go throw out all the bread, then we won't have enough for breakfast, so Mom will have to take us to the bagel shop for breakfast before school."

Trump card. Macy loved bagels.

I unlocked the front door for my sister, and before I started emptying the turkey meat from its container, she'd returned, ready for her next mission. I handed her all but one piece of turkey meat, then jammed the almost-empty pack back into the fridge. Next, I gave her a ton of apples, then a bunch of cheese, then six eggs, telling her to be careful not to break them as she dashed out to the garbage bins.

She took orders extraordinary well.

We dumped the rest of the cereal, threw out most of the pretzels, and jettisoned the last two bananas. When it was time for breakfast that morning, my mom opened the fridge, scratched her head, and said, "I swear you kids are eating me out of house and home. There's nothing for breakfast. What do you say we grab bagels on the way to school?"

"Great idea, Mom." I smiled at my co-conspirator.

"Great idea," Macy seconded.

We gave each other a high five as we walked out the door.

Grocery Antics

20

I told Nathan everything during recess. Even if he couldn't fight alongside me, he could coach us on certain matters. And there was a particular matter—a specific plan of attack—that needed his help.

He nodded and listened and then said, "Let's go find your sister right now, and I can show her."

"But we'd have to go to the Baby Lot," I said.

"Doesn't matter. This is war. And a good soldier knows you sometimes have to venture into dangerous territory."

The kindergartners, first graders, and second graders have their own playground, and the bigger kids call it the Baby Lot. It was an unwritten rule among third, fourth, and fifth graders that stepping foot on the Baby Lot made you a baby. No one wanted to be a baby, so no big kid ever even placed a toe on the Baby Lot.

I felt like a spy heading into enemy territory, glancing behind us several times to make sure no one recorded our mission on hidden camera. We stayed by the gate, our feet firmly on the big kid border, and called Macy over.

She sprinted to the gate in two seconds flat.

"Macy, Nathan needs to show you how to throw like a champ," I told her.

"Hi, Nathan!" She waved even though he was right next to her.

Nathan pulled her aside, then demonstrated some baseball throws. Macy didn't play baseball, but she was such a natural at sports, she picked up the technique quickly. That night's battle was going to require some serious chucking power.

After they finished their quick recess lesson, I whispered the rest of the plan to her. She nodded, but this time I knew her nods were real. She understood the seriousness of the situation. Nathan and I returned to class.

"Thanks for helping," I said.

"That's what friends are for. Now, go kick some squirrel zombie butt tonight and tell me everything tomorrow. I want every single battle detail." He chopped the air one more time before the bell rang.

At the grocery store, my mom wheeled a cart down the fruit aisle first, like she usually did. Macy and I started arguing, like we usually did, only this time our fight was pre-planned.

"I want to ride on the back of the cart," Macy shouted.

"I never get to. You always get to," I whined, as she grabbed hold of the cart. I tried to hop on too, elbowing her.

"Ben, you're too big for that," my mom scolded.

"Can I push then?"

"Sure."

I took over the reins. I bumped into the bananas, knocking a bunch over; steered Macy into the oranges, toppling five or six; and crashed into the apples, sending a pair of bright-red Macintoshes rolling across the grocery store floor. I put my hand over my mouth, doing my best to look *contrite*—that's how my mom likes me to feel when I'm not nice to Macy, *contrite*—and said, "Oops."

My mom rolled her eyes. "I'll push the cart."

That was a good start. But we had to achieve more parental exasperation.

Macy implemented the second part of the plan as she held on to the back of the cart. She let go with one hand and one foot and leaned out, like a trapeze artist swinging. She switched quickly to her left, then her right, then left again, while singing, "I can sing, I can fly off a shopping cart."

My mom shook her head and started to say something, but she didn't have time to deal with Macy's aerial antics, because I teed up some rapid-fire questions.

"Can we get pineapple?" I tossed a container of pre-cut pineapple into the cart. "What about blueberries?" I blurted out and added a carton to the basket. "Oh, look! They have raspberries. I haven't had raspberries in forever, and they're my favorite thing. Mom, can we please, please, please have raspberries?"

I dropped down on my knees and clasped my hands together for effect.

Macy jumped off the cart and joined me. "Please, please, please, please."

"Enough! Why don't you guys run off to the cereal aisle to get some Toasted Os? Meet me by the milk in five minutes."

We bolted, and then whizzed past the cereal section, the chips, the flour, the bread, the frozen goods, the rice, and the paper towels. We only had eyes for the toy aisle.

"Let's get three bags, just to be safe," I said.

Macy grabbed the supplies, handing the bags to me. We hurried away from the toys and into the express checkout lane. There were two people ahead of us.

"C'mon, C'mon. Move faster," I whispered. Then to Macy, "Conduct an aisle scan, please."

A stealthy spy, Macy slid around the magazines to peer out. She popped back a second later and gave a curt nod. She was good at this, I had to admit. She took directions well and executed like a pro. When the woman in front of me argued about the price of a pepper, my heart started to beat faster and my nerves skyrocketed. I tapped my foot as the cashier checked the price. "Go grab those Toasted Os and meet me right back here," I said to Macy, because we couldn't return to Mom empty-handed. Macy took off.

Finally, it was my turn to check out, and I thrust the battle supplies into the cashier's hands. I grabbed from my pocket a crumpled five-dollar bill I'd snagged from my allowance jar that morning.

"Someone's going to have a lot of fun," the cashier said, chuckling so loudly he might as well have had a microphone. I bet my mom could hear him all the way in the fruit aisle. "That'll be $3.78."

I gave him the five-dollar bill. "No bag, please." I jammed the purchase into my back pocket.

"Now, sonny, how much change am I supposed to give you?" he said in that voice adults use when they think they have to teach kids every single second of the day.

I was no idiot. I knew exactly how much change was needed. "One dollar and twenty-two cents."

He dropped the change into my hand as Macy returned, landing like a cartoon character, in a swirl of dust. She held a box of Toasted Os in her hands.

"Nice work, Macy." I draped my arm over her shoulder.

"Thanks, Ben." She placed her arm around my waist. "We're a good team."

We strolled back to the milk aisle. Macy showed Mom the cereal, then dropped the box in our shopping cart. Mom raised an eyebrow, then smiled.

She was pleased with our cereal retrieval. I was pleased with our water-balloon purchase.

21

Project Wet Squirrel

My mom likes me to be active. That doesn't mean I have to do sports, because obviously sports aren't in the cards for me. But she wants me to exercise—walk the dog, ride a bike, or run around the yard.

"Normal kid stuff. Running, jumping, climbing. It's vital for kids with this kind of CP to do. It helps keep you strong," she says.

So I'd learned the third-best way to get on my mom's good side—after being nice to Macy and volunteering to go to bed early—was to play outside. The bonus—whenever I told my mom I'd be playing outside, she was so happy she'd leave me alone. That's what we needed today.

"We need more tinfoil! And plastic wrap!"

"I'll go get some!"

"Remember, what are you going to say if Mom sees you?"

"We're building a trench for a science experiment," Macy repeated our cover. "We want to see how much water it can hold before it needs a dam."

"Excellent. Now go."

She sprang up the stairs and into the kitchen, while I dug a deeper trench. I didn't know if my plan would work, especially since the zombie squirrels I had in my

96

yard didn't behave like the ones Nigel had battled. But they did act like cats, and I was going to treat them like zombie cats and target their weakness.

And what is a cat's biggest weakness?

Water.

Cats hate water.

Footsteps pounded loudly upstairs. Mom arrived on the deck to inspect. "What exactly are you two doing?"

Macy held her hands up, giving Mom an *I-Told-You-So* look. "I told you we were building a trench. And you didn't believe me. But see, there it is. Right before your very eyes." Macy held out her hand like a magician presenting a rabbit from a hat, showcasing the six-foot long and one-foot wide trench we'd dug from the bottom of the stairs into the yard.

"You told me you were going to be playing soccer."

"We *were* playing soccer, and now we're building a trench, and we're lining it with foil as a base, then plastic wrap to seal in the water so it doesn't soak into the dirt. Is there a law against expressing a spirit of scientific exploration?" I said.

Mom laughed. "I suppose not, my little scientists. Especially when you put it that way. So, what are you learning about trenches?"

"We will issue a full report after we test it out."

"All righty then. I guess I'll make dinner."

Macy and I finished lining the trench with its double protective coatings, and then I pulled the hose over. Macy turned on the water and we watched the trench fill up. We turned the water off and stared at the trench for the next few minutes as if we were burning holes in it with our laser eyes.

The water held!

I hoped it'd hold for the next six hours until the squirrel zombies rose up from their underground bunkers. Part of me was tempted to grab the hose and spray the holes now, like a crazed fireman dousing an evil fire. But I had a feeling that would qualify as "improper" zombie disposal. And improper disposal meant one thing—they'd come back bigger and badder.

We had to do this the right way. We had to follow the rules.

"One down. Two to go. Lieutenant Macy, please retrieve the deer sprinkler."

"Sir, yes sir." She darted off into the shed and materialized seconds later with a sprinkler head that erupted if something moved in front of it—a perfect stealth weapon to battle those dastardly creatures. I placed the sprinkler on the ground. We needed to use the hose to fill the water balloons, so I'd attach the sprinkler after we prepped.

"Macy, is the parental authority figure safely in the kitchen?"

"Sir, yes sir."

"Do you see any signs she might be coming out?"

"Sir, no sir."

"I will alert you for action if I hear her. Commence project water balloon."

Macy retrieved a cooler-sized plastic bin from the storage shed. We lugged the bin underneath the steps, spent the next twenty minutes filling it with our water-balloon weapons, and snapped the cover on. I glanced back at the yard and shivered, knowing soon the ground would erupt with some of the freakiest animal zombies of all.

A Good Excuse

22

Here's the thing. You can only use a good excuse once on an adult. Use it twice, and they'll know you're up to something. So slipping a newspaper onto Mom's pillow to make her drowsy wasn't going to cut it tonight. I chose a different strategy to induce an early bedtime for Mom. We couldn't battle squirrel zombies with her tapping away on her latest research report late at night, so I had to cut her fuel line.

As she helped Macy pick out jammies, I quietly grabbed some Benadryl tablets from my medicine cabinet and stuffed them into my pocket. When Macy asked my mom to brush her hair, I sneaked into the kitchen and swapped out my mom's regular coffee for my dad's decaf mix. I didn't want my mom consuming even an ounce of caffeine to keep her up. Next, I crushed the pills with the end of a fork. My mom used to give me Benadryl when I was little and would fly on a plane. She called them sleepy pills. Evidently, I conked out the second I consumed them. Since I have no memory of any plane trips, I guess she was right.

So how could she blame me for spiking her coffee when I'd learned the trick from her? But as I was about to stir the pills into her coffee mix, I stopped. What if Benadryl was dangerous to my mom? I didn't know a thing about this *sleepy pill*. My heart sank with worry. Even if she didn't believe me about squirrel zombies, I would never ever hurt her. I dumped the pills into the trashcan.

But I still didn't plan on letting her drink full-strength coffee tonight. I left the decaf mix in her coffee maker. I'd simply have to wait for the *lack* of caffeine to put her to sleep.

At 9:00 she brewed a pot. At 9:05 she took her first sip. At 9:10 she started yawning. At 9:15 she couldn't stop yawning. By 9:30, she'd crashed on her bed on top of the covers.

Perfect. My mom was a caffeine junkie and I'd successfully deprived her. Just to be safe though, I grabbed the noise machine from their closet, plugged it in, and turned on some relaxing ocean waves to drown out any sounds of the outdoors tonight.

She was in the cocoon of a peaceful sea breeze.

I changed out of my pajamas and back into jeans, a sweatshirt, and sneakers. I crept out of my bedroom, tiptoed down the hall, and walked quietly onto the deck. The door creaked as I shut it. For a fraction of a second, I feared it would lock, and I'd be stuck waiting for the meowing squirrels alone.

A cool breeze swept by, bringing along a handful of leaves, like that first night. Had Percy started early? Was he already calling forth his undead friends?

I had locked him in Macy's room and planned to keep him there until midnight. I knew I'd have to free him then, and it pained me to think about it. Taking him out worked last night as a stall tactic, but I'd have to end the war fair and square tonight. To do that, the zombies would need their cross-species living leader.

But for now he was caged, and I needed to finish preparations.

I walked down the steps and underneath the stairs. I tried to find my way in the dark, ducking my head as I reached for the bin stuffed full of water balloons. But I banged my forehead on the underside of the steps. "Ouch," I said, rubbing my palm against the spot. I sucked in my breath and soldiered on, grabbing the bin with both hands. I dragged it out from its hiding place, across a stretch of grass, and to the bottom of the long flight of steps, probably twelve or so.

I started hauling it up the stairs.

Bump.

The bin smacked the first step loudly, like a clap of thunder. I couldn't risk Mom hearing it. I grabbed the bin and hoisted it up into my arms. A balloon bounced out and splattered on a step, dousing it. Darn. But that was a casualty of war, and I'd have to let it go.

The bin was heavy and hard to carry. But I pictured Captain Sparkles meowing, and I had all the strength in the world. I carried it to the deck without dropping it. Next, I flipped our picnic table on its side, forming a barricade. I placed the bin of balloons behind it.

I surveyed the quiet battlefield one final time. It was still. Too still. I returned to the house, pulling the door shut. I assumed my spot next to the dog door and set my alarm clock for ten minutes to midnight.

Then I fell asleep wearing my jeans, sweatshirt, and sneakers, with my braces on.

My full battle gear.

23

Don't Mess With the Claw

When I woke up, my first thought was that a bomb had landed in my lap. But it was the white plastic dog-door cover, and it was broken in two, both pieces resting across my legs. My sister gestured wildly at the dog door. "I swear, Ben, it was like he flew out of my room. I got up to go to the bathroom and he ran!"

It took me a second to realize she was talking about Percy. "I didn't mean to let him out," Macy said, and her lips quivered. Tears would roll next. She felt horrible for letting him escape early, but I realized this was my mistake. "It's not your fault, Macy. I should have locked him in his cat carrier instead of your room. Don't worry about it, okay?"

She sucked in a sob and pulled herself together.

I picked up the pieces of the dog door and placed them on the floor, then peered out onto the deck. Percy was nowhere to be seen. I looked back at the severed remains of the door and saw a cat's claw marks clear across the plastic. I shivered, knowing Percy had sliced the door in half with his claw to escape, so desperate was he to command his unearthly friends. What else would he do with his cat claws?

I shook my head briefly, wondering how our cat could have turned on us. But the cat's motives didn't matter right now. The battle was about to begin.

I glanced at my sister. She wore her purple flannel pajamas with cartoon cats on them, but her feet were bare.

"Macy. Shoes," I instructed. "Be super quiet, and double check that my door is shut."

I didn't want my dog near those breath-sucking roadkill ghouls. Macy tiptoed back to her room to fetch her sneakers. I opened the back door so I could take my position behind the table. Then I heard Macy gently shutting my door, followed by the sound of Captain Sparkles trotting down the hall. She'd gotten out! How could Macy have let her out? She knew we needed to keep the dog safe.

"She slipped out when I checked on her!" Macy looked like she was going to cry.

Captain Sparkles was in dog mode this time, and she raced through the living room, her nails scraping against the floor. I lunged to grab her, but she darted outside, her ears tucked against her head. She rushed to the edge of the deck and poked her head through the slats to stare into the yard.

Then the barking began. The day away from the zombies must have restored a little more dog traits to her, but even though I was glad she could bark, I didn't want my mom to hear her. "Captain Sparkles! No rude barking."

The most amazing thing happened. She stopped barking. Just like that. No questions asked, no begging, no pleading. I'd never given her a command before, but it worked. It really worked!

"Now, go inside." I pointed to the back door. But I realized I couldn't send her inside. There was no longer

a cover for the dog door to keep her inside the house. And judging from the way the leaves floated and twisted around the cartoon cats on Macy's pajama pants, I didn't have time to lock the dog in her crate.

I'd have to keep her by my side and fight one-handed. I grabbed her collar and held her tight. With my other hand, I grabbed for Macy, gripping her little fingers in my big-brother hand. "Stay close to me," I whispered, then I tipped my chin to the yard, where leaves and dirt swirled together. I watched the nearby tree, waiting for Percy to leap down again. But he didn't bother with the theatrics. He was all business as he sauntered from behind a bush and casually waved a paw in the air.

Macy peeked through the railing and saw the same scene unfold that I had witnessed the other night. As Percy waved his strangely powerful paw, his undead minions rose from the ground, their glassy eyes staring at us. They looked different than the first night. More alive. Their eyes were no longer empty. They looked around, as if they could see everything, like cats in the night. They started to walk, and they weren't so clunky anymore. They were almost graceful, as if they had evolved from roadkill squirrels to agile cats.

And, of course, that's what Nigel had tried to teach me. Animal zombies moved quickly. They evolved quickly. Even animal zombies raised by a different living animal.

Macy backed up into me. "I'm scared."

"It's okay," I said, but I wondered if it really was. I'd gotten my sister involved, my friend involved, my dog involved, when maybe I should have insisted on involving our mom. I should have grabbed her by the hand and shown her the zombies last night. But now, she was out cold, and nothing would wake her up. And who was I kidding, thinking I could take on zombie squirrels?

Drip. Drip. Drip.

I followed the sound.

The answer was right before me at the bottom of the steps. The hose! I'd forgotten to attach the deer sprinkler to the end of it when our mom called us into dinner. But I didn't need a tricky trench, a stealthy deer sprinkler, or even a bin full of water balloons. I'd just turn on the hose and spray those squirrelly furballs into zombie oblivion. The end of the hose dripped into the trench, where I'd left it earlier.

"Macy! I know how to beat them!" The beady-eyed gray squirrel marched across the yard. "You don't have to be scared. We can do this. I've been over-thinking this, adding too many weapons. But all I need to do is spray them directly. So I have to go down the steps and turn on the water faucet," I explained, because the faucet was at the bottom of the stairs. "You stand behind the picnic table and man the water-balloon station. Wait till I give you the command, and when I do, just lob them at any furball that makes it past the trench, like Nathan showed you. And hold Captain Sparkles tight *the whole time*."

Macy nodded, wrapped her hand around the dog's collar, and scurried behind the table. I ran as fast as I could to the stairs while I kept my eyes on the squirrel zombies, their tire-tread marks visible even in the dark. They formed a line and continued their march across the yard, their tails swishing like cat tails. I clomped down the steps, holding tight to the railing. *Just one foot after the other, don't try to go too fast*, I told myself. My braces-laden feet clunked against the wood steps. But it was dark, so I didn't see the small puddle on the bottom step. I slipped on the leftovers from the water balloon that had fallen out of the bin earlier and landed smack on my butt on the concrete landing, my feet sliding all the way into the trench at the bottom of the stairs.

My shoes were soaked. My socks were soaked. I couldn't do anything without tripping or falling. But there was no time to whine, so I pushed myself up as the squirrel zombies edged closer. The gray one was a few feet away, the tawny one mere inches behind him. I started twisting the faucet handle. "C'mon, C'mon," I said to myself, each crank taking ages it seemed.

"You okay?" Macy called out from above because she couldn't see me anymore. "Do you want me to throw a balloon yet?"

"No. I've almost got it."

The gray squirrel took another step. I twisted more, and the hose began to gurgle, the water slowly trickling through it. He took another step. Another gurgle.

I yanked the hose, pulling it closer to me. At the same time, the beady-eyed gray squirrel crossed the last patch of grass before the stairs, then plunged into the waiting trench at the bottom of the steps. Everything went silent for a few seconds. All the zombies stopped moving. I froze in place. They cast their eyes on the trench, which had started to bubble and sizzle, like it was boiling over. The sounds grew louder and sharper.

Then there was a huge *POP*!

The gray squirrel was gone. Like a fat balloon popping, he left behind only a few strands of matted gray fur. So that's what the *pop* was all about. Animal zombies popped and then disappeared, leaving only a few pieces of fur. Zombie remains weren't too messy after all.

"One down!" I pressed hard on the hose, angling my thumb over the end to make the water spray. I aimed it straight at the tawny squirrel, but I stopped when I heard another *pop*. The gray fur pieces from the first creature were gone, and in their place was a squirrel. A living, breathing, scampering squirrel.

I shook my head, then stared hard at the squirrel, alive and twitchy. The squirrel took a quick look at me, then turned tail and raced across the yard and up into a tree. I blinked and was sure I'd just seen a mirage. The living squirrel must have been just that—a living squirrel checking out the nighttime action.

I returned to my task as the skinny tawny undead one walked to the edge of the trench. I took aim, watching as a huge spray of water shot over my thumb and out of the hose. Another moment of silence. Another bubble, sizzle, and another *pop*.

"Only eleven to go!" I said to Macy.

I pointed the hose at a threesome next, a couple of brown fluffy squirrels and a small gray one with a white belly. Then I stopped when a tawny squirrel leapt out of the trench. It wasn't the zombie squirrel; it was a living version of the once-undead creature.

Whoa. My mind felt like it was bending, because this was seriously freaky.

The roadkill zombies were coming back to life. The water somehow was releasing them.

Release.

I remembered that word from Nigel's handbook. Do remember, except in the rare occasions where a release is possible, a pop is always the goal.

These squirrel zombies weren't just popping. They were popping and then coming back to life. They were being released to their living states. Something clicked, and I suddenly got it. They had a second chance at life, these squirrels. They were roadkill; they'd died before their time, died unnatural deaths. So rather than becoming zombie remains when they popped, they became alive again. That was their release.

I watched as the tawny squirrel scurried away, like a regular, living squirrel.

This was cool, and I needed to get back to work zapping the others, because I was helping them, too. I pressed my thumb against the end of the hose, ready to blast them back to life with my zombie-splattering weapon of awesomeness. But one of the brown fluffy squirrels had other plans. He jumped across the trench, reached out a little paw and unveiled a mighty set of claws, swiping one across the hose. He trailed his claw, carving open the hose. The squirrels were still dangerous when they were in their zombie form—all the more reason to release them. Their claws were like the steely kitchen knives used on cooking shows. I stared down at my hose, now useless as a weapon. The brown fluffy one hadn't even gotten wet. The hose simply spluttered through the slashes the squirrel made, dribbling little streams of water.

Eleven undead, armed, and dangerous zombie squirrels imitated the jumper. They leapt over the trench one by one and marched up the steps to my deck.

Wait. Make that eleven zombie squirrels and one cat zombie. Because at the end of the line there was a new creature, and he wasn't a squirrel of any sort. He was the tiniest little undead cat. A kitten zombie.

He was really cute too. I sure hoped he'd be released back to true kittendom after I splattered his furry face with water.

A Cry for Help

24

"**M**acy! Time for the balloons."

I started up the steps, keeping close to the house. I didn't want to touch any of the squirrel creatures accidentally.

But they didn't care about me. They didn't try to attack me with their vicious claws or inhale my air or suck my life force. They just went, up, up, up. Macy held the dog's collar tightly in one hand and a water balloon in her other hand, poised behind the table. When the first one appeared in Macy's range, she cocked her arm back and said, "Take that!"

She was like a Major League pitcher! She'd picked up the skills in only one five-minute lesson with Nathan. The red water balloon flew across the deck and smashed into the brown fluffy squirrel's chest, turning him into a few strands of fur.

"Way to go, Macy! Keep it up."

Seconds later, a brown fluffy squirrel materialized in his place and ran off into the night. Released from roadkill, turned back to life.

I raced ahead of the squirrels and ducked behind our barricade as Macy fired off another balloon, then another, taking down two chubby gray squirrels, who popped, then returned to life. My sister was amazing! I vowed to attend every single baseball game she'd ever play in her life and cheer the loudest. She had an arm of steel, and a hand that wouldn't let go of our dog, even as Captain Sparkles snarled and tried to nip at the zombies.

"Eight to go! No, nine," I corrected as I remembered the zombie kitten. I dipped my hand into the bin, grabbed a fat yellow water balloon and used it to take out a dark brown squirrel. I plucked out a blue water balloon and lobbed it at another squirrel. But I hit my dog instead, just as I heard Macy cry, "Captain Sparkles!"

Oh no! She was supposed to be hiding behind the table. My sister must have been pelting zombies so hard that her grip on the dog's collar had loosened. Captain Sparkles had broken away, and there she was, rushing straight into the middle of the squirrel zombies, nudging them with her nose, nipping at their nasty little undead legs, trying to get them away from us.

No!

The problem was she'd herded the zombies, like sheep, through the open dog door, past my sister and into the living room. The dog part of her was still working as she clustered the zombie squirrels into a corner by the door. They glared at her, then swiveled their heads to stare at the deck, waiting for something, waiting for an order. I followed their eyes to Percy, perched serenely on the deck railing. From his command post as the living cat leader of a pack of feline-like zombie squirrels, he nodded down at them and they understood his directive immediately.

They meowed in unison, then the squirrel zombies leaned into Captain Sparkles and sucked in their breath, inhaling the air around her. She backed away from them, but they came closer, their foul, rattling mouths hunting out hers. They knocked her down on the floor.

"No!" I grabbed balloons from the bin, but they spilled from my arms and broke on the deck.

"I'll do it," Macy said. She grabbed two balloons, yanked the door open and leapt into the house in one fluid, fast motion. I needed her speed now more than ever. She catapulted a balloon into the melee, nicking the back paw of a zombie. It wasn't a direct hit, so the squirrel kept sucking.

Macy dropped the remaining balloon, flung herself into the pile of squirrel zombies and reached for Captain's collar, tugging and pulling to free our dog.

"Get off my Captain Sparkles!" Macy grabbed two squirrels with zig-zag tire tracks down their bellies. They didn't try to suck her breath. They only wanted the canine.

I looked around frantically for more weapons, more water. Then I noticed the dog's water bowl on the deck. It was full, so I grabbed it and carried it inside and placed it on the floor as some water sloshed over the rim. I motioned frantically to Macy. We thrust the pair of mangy furballs into the bowl and they quickly popped. Seconds later, two springy squirrels emerged from the water, assessed the situation, and hightailed it out of our house. We were down to six as Macy freed Captain Sparkles and pulled her away from the remaining zombies.

Then Percy sprang down off the railing and bounced into the house.

Captain Sparkles spotted him, twitched her tail several times, then lunged for him, like a cat playing with a playmate. But our dog was bigger and stronger, and she knocked him down hard. Percy lay sprawled on his back, his cat paws up in the air, helpless or so it seemed, as he mewed like a wounded kitten.

The dog hovered above him.

It was an all-too familiar pose. A pose I'd seen so many times. Captain Sparkles pinning Percy. Percy being the victim. But Captain Sparkles wasn't chasing Percy this time. She wasn't harassing him or making his life miserable. She was protecting Macy and me from the enemy.

Percy let out another sad, plaintive meow. Not the meow he'd used to call forth his troops two nights ago. But a real cat's meow, like the sound they made when they were stuck somewhere, when they were hungry, when they needed help.

When they needed help.

That's when it all hit me.

Nigel said a living cat could command an army of zombies under two conditions—there had to be an unnatural hole. Check. We had that. And two, the cat had a need. An *emotional* need. The cat needed help.

Percy was a troublemaker, Percy was annoying, but Percy also needed our help. And Percy had been trying to tell us that all along. That's why he'd called the zombies. He didn't have a choice. We weren't helping him. We weren't training the dog to be nice to him or even to stop jumping on him. And who wants to be chased all day? Who wants to be attacked all day? No one.

I knew what to do.

"Captain Sparkles. *Off*," I called out in the sternest, strongest, dog-training-est voice I could muster, the same voice I'd used earlier when she'd escaped onto the deck.

She backed away from Percy. She sat down on her butt and stayed still. I realized, then, that I could train her, and she could listen. I was good at something after all.

But I had a cat as well as a dog, and my cat looked scared still. "Is this what you want, Percy? Do you want me to protect you too? To train you?"

He didn't answer me, of course. But somehow, I think he understood, especially when I reached for him, picked him up in my arms, and petted him between the ears. He didn't hiss or scratch or bare his fang at me. He let me pick him up and take care of him, because I was finally treating him nicely too. I hadn't been a good pet owner to Percy. But that would change. I would treat the cat and the dog the same. "I'll keep you safe, too."

But there was still that little problem of those hungry squirrel creatures of the night in my living room. They were ready to suck Captain Sparkles's every last breath and make her a cat in dog's clothing. They zeroed in on her again, mouths open, until Percy leapt out of my arms and into the middle of his army. He stuck out his arm, revealed a claw and he poked each of his minions. One poke per cat-like squirrel.

Pop.

Pop.

Pop.

Pop.

Pop.

Pop.

I couldn't wait to tell Nigel there was another way to beat a cross-species zombie. Win the leader's loyalty and the use of his claw.

Within seconds, there were six living squirrels in our house. Six squirrels whose lives had ended too soon, under the wheel of a car, who now had new lives. Percy didn't even try to chase them. He simply stood and watched them return to the wild of the backyard.

Donuts at Last

There was one creature Percy didn't poke with his claw. The kitten zombie. Instead, he sniffed it, then bent down and licked the kitten zombie's head. The kitten zombie looked up at Percy and purred the loudest purr I'd ever heard. I stared in complete and utter amazement because Percy was licking a zombie. Percy was cleaning a zombie.

Then I smacked my palm against my forehead. Of course he wasn't cleaning a zombie. He was cleaning a real, live kitten. But just to be sure, I asked Macy to grab a cup of water from the kitchen, and we poured it over the kitten. "It's important to double-check these things," I said as we doused the little feline in water.

Nothing happened. There was no sizzle, no pop, no explosion into just a few threads of fur. Sure, the kitten got wet and started to meow, but Percy lapped the water off the kitten's wet head.

The kitten was just a kitten.

"Do you think Mom will let us keep him? He's so, so, so cute."

"He is pretty cute," I said. "I think we should call him Nigel the Cat."

Macy clapped her hands and petted the kitten. "Nigel the Cat! Hello, Nigel the Cat."

I turned around to check on the dog. She was wagging her tail as if she were competing in a tail-wagging contest. Then she jumped on me, put her front paws on my shoulders and gave me a big old lick across the cheek. She was back—totally one-hundred-percent back to normal. We had saved the dog. And we'd given thirteen roadkill squirrels a second chance at a happy life.

The great thing about animal zombies was that clean-up was a cinch. No mangled, oozing bodies. No furry limbs splattered across the yard. We cleaned up the water balloons and threw out the unused ones, popping them with a pin. I moved the bin back to the shed and propped the table upright. There was nothing to be done about the damaged hose, so we left it on the deck and went inside. I didn't know what to do about the broken dog-door cover, so I left it on the floor.

"You were a good partner, Macy."

She yawned. "Those squirrels were pretty yucky. I wouldn't let them in for tea." Then she kicked off her sneakers, crawled into bed, and fell asleep. Percy jumped onto her bed and curled up next to her. Nigel the Cat joined them, cuddling up to Percy, who rested a paw protectively across the kitten's chest. Percy's eyes were no longer glassy. He seemed like a normal cat again. Well, as normal as Percy would ever be. Captain Sparkles followed me and tucked herself into a dog ball at the foot of my bed. The dog and the cat weren't best friends and probably never would be. But I had a good feeling there'd be peace among the pets, and I would be nice to both the dog and the cats.

When I woke up on Saturday morning, my mom stood in the hallway and took a long drink from her coffee mug. "Boy, am I still zonked. I think I fell asleep before ten last night, and I didn't wake up once. I don't think anything could have woken me up last night."

I smiled. "Nothing *could* wake you up. Because Captain got stuck outside last night and wound up smashing through the dog door to get back in. I found it split in two." I figured the dog wouldn't mind taking one for the team.

"Really? That's so strange. But then again, strange things do happen at night."

That was for sure. Then we showed her Nigel the Cat, and she said we could keep him.

When my dad returned from his trip a few hours later, he took me out for that chocolate glazed donut, as promised. We usually went alone—him and me. But I insisted on bringing Macy this time.

"I'm impressed, Ben. I think it's really great you wanted to bring your sister," he said as we pulled up to the bakery, which happened to be right next to the Halloween Hideout.

"She can be cool sometimes, Dad."

Macy gave me a knowing smile and placed her finger to her lips. We had a secret, and we were going to keep it.

"Dad, can I meet you in the bakery in two minutes? I want to check on one thing for my costume."

My dad nodded, and I walked into Halloween Hideout, heading straight for the back.

"Nigel?"

"Is that Ben or a zombie hunter I hear?" Nigel pulled back the curtain. "I take it you survived to tell the tale?" I gave him the highlights. "I'm going to need you to write a new chapter in my field guide."

"Speaking of your field guide, there were a bunch of torn-out pages in the copy I had."

Nigel raised an eyebrow, then nodded thoughtfully, as if what I'd said was the final piece in a puzzle.

"That makes sense actually. That copy had been loaned out by a co-worker to his good mate, and I suspect that good mate may have ripped out those pages. Because I did a little digging into the previous infestation, the one from the summer, and it turns out it occurred at Danny Summerfield's house. Does that name ring a bell?"

"Danny Summerfield! He's our handyman. He installed our dog door."

"That's what I thought. That was *his* dog door. He bought it for his dog, only he wound up letting squirrel zombies in through it, and he failed to dispose of them properly. He used a net and stuffed them back into the earth."

"And then he passed that door on to us," I jumped in, putting two and two together. "Which explains why my mom thought she was getting a steel door, because she asked for a steel door but he gave us his plastic dog door instead. He was passing his problem on to us. I'm going to tell my mom we need a new handyman. That weasel!"

"Such a shame too, to learn of him taking shortcuts when the answers were there in black and white in the book." Nigel shook his head, *tsk-tsking* Danny. "But there's more. Evidently, that door isn't just for zombies. It's a very special make and model that has its own sort of magic."

"Magic? We're talking about magic now?"

"Yes, and here's a little hint. Next time you have chicken for dinner, try tossing a bone through the dog door."

"A chicken bone? Why?"

"Chickens have some very interesting relatives," Nigel said.

"They're related to dinosaurs. We learned that in science class this year. You're not saying I can make dinosaurs un-extinct with that door, are you?"

Nigel shrugged. "I don't know. I've never tried. But it might be fun to see."

I wasn't so sure a back yard full of dinosaurs would be fun. But it *would* be interesting.

Even if I wanted to cavort with the dinos, I'd have to convince my mom to keep that plastic dog door. And I'd fought enough battles for one week.

For now, I wanted my donut, so I said goodbye and joined my dad and sister next door. The chocolate glaze was every bit as good as I'd hoped, and I decided to put cats and dinosaurs and dog doors out of my mind for the rest of the day.

Acknowledgements

Big huge slobbery happy-dog kisses go to all the people who made this possible: my editor Trisha, who was so much fun to work with and who gives the BEST comments, smiley faces, and anecdotes; my agent Michelle, who rolls with the crazy; the amazingly talented Slake for her fantastic designs; and the entire team at Spencer Hill for believing in this story. Lots of bones and kibble for the best dogs in the world—Violet and Flipper McDoodle. And most of all, thank you to my family—to my husband, who brings me lattes to keep me writing, and to my children, who are the loves of my life and who inspired this story.

About the Author

Daisy Whitney is also the author of the young adult novels *The Mockingbirds*, *The Rivals*, *When You Were Here*, and *Starry Nights*. Her books have received critical acclaim, including NPR Best Teen Read, ABC New Voices Pick, ALA Best Fiction for Young Adults, an NCIBA Book of the Year Honorable Mention, a *Romantic Times* Best of YA, and a Chicago Public Library Best of the Best. Daisy was inspired to write *Ben Fox: Squirrel Zombie Specialist At Your Service* one chilly fall night when her dog bounded through the dog door carrying a bone the size of a baseball bat that she'd dug up in the backyard. The next day Daisy, a self-described scaredy cat, boarded up the dog door and started writing *Ben Fox* for her fearless grade-school son.

CPSIA information can be obtained at www.ICGtesting.com
Printed in the USA
LVOW08s0512170914

404456LV00002B/2/P